D1561413

The Tempting Minx

Fate of the Worthingtons

Laura A. Barnes

To my husband:
I love you more than words can say

The Tempting Minx

Chapter One

MAGGIE WORTHINGTON SAT SIDEWAYS with her legs hanging over the arm of the chair, swinging them back and forth. How much longer must she endure listening to her mother plan her debut? Hopefully the torture would end soon. She longed to slide into her breeches and ride her horse, Penelope. The days of idling her time away with lengthy rides across the estate and helping in the stables with the horses would end once she reached London.

When she turned eighteen last year, her world had come to a crashing halt. However, her sister-in-law, Evelyn, had taken pity on her and convinced her mother to wait another year before they presented Maggie to society.

Her mother realized if Maggie's entrance was successful, then it would be difficult to find grooms for her older sisters, Eden and Noel, since they had yet to wed. But after a year, Noel found herself engaged, and her mother refused to wait any longer for Maggie to have a season. Her mother feared the longer Maggie remained out of society, the more difficult it would be for her to tame her daughter's carefree behavior.

Even now, her mother glared her disapproval at her abandoned manners. Maggie imagined her mother reprimanding her. *Margaret Ann, sit like a proper lady this instant.*

When her mother arched an eyebrow, Maggie sat up straight and placed her feet on the floor. She brushed out her skirts and smiled serenely at her mother. Her mother nodded her approval and continued her conversation with Evelyn.

Evelyn offered Maggie a kind smile, understanding her behavior because Evelyn's sister Charlotte Sinclair, Charlie to her family and friends, suffered the same affliction as Maggie. She longed for the open skies and fresh air. Evelyn was Maggie's biggest supporter, showing her mother and older brother Reese how they should handle Maggie differently than Eden and Noel. Her other brother, Graham, helped whenever he came to visit to keep them from making her into a proper lady. She missed him, and he was the only promising aspect of her upcoming visit to London.

"Gam, Gam, Gam," Mina chanted, toddling into the parlor.

Maggie swept Mina into her arms. "Yes, I miss Graham too."

Mina pointed at the door and kept singing, "Gam, Gam, Gam."

Everyone laughed at her silliness. Evelyn held out her arms, and Maggie passed Mina off. Her niece's arrival gave Maggie the perfect distraction to sneak away. Evelyn and Reese's daughter, her mother's only grandchild, kept her mother occupied enough to forget about her youngest child. Maggie must remember to reward Mina with a biscuit later.

She started backing out of the parlor, prepared to stop if anyone caught her, and almost made her escape when she bumped into somebody.

"Sneaking away, are you, squirt?" Graham whispered in her ear.

Maggie turned around, squealing her excitement. "Graham!" She threw herself into his arms.

Graham swung his sister around, laughing at her greeting. "Glad to see you, too."

"Save me," she whispered.

Graham chuckled. "Ahh, still dramatic, I see."

"They are planning my debut."

Graham gasped in shock. "How dare they?"

Maggie punched him in the arm once she realized he held no sympathy for her. "Not you too."

"It is past time, my dear."

Maggie scowled. "If your intention is not to help save me, then what is the reason for your visit?"

Graham gave her a devious smile. "Why, to join the torture."

Maggie punched him again and returned to her seat to sulk. It wasn't until her mother greeted her brother that she noticed Graham wasn't alone. A gentleman stood by his side, watching Graham interact with his family. When he noticed Maggie's gaze on him, he winked at her before returning his attention to her mother while Graham made the introductions.

Maggie wasn't one to blush, but her face grew warm from the gentleman's bold stare. Throughout the years, she'd spent time with a variety of men, from a gentleman to a stable hand. Granted, her brothers or some member of Evelyn's family were always present, and the encounters revolved around horseflesh. However, none of them had affected her senses as this stranger.

He held himself with confidence and found amusement in her family's antics. He even wore a warm smile when Mina captured everyone's attention again with her chant about her uncle. Maggie's gaze drifted over his features, and she noted his firm chin, dark hair that he kept cut short, a smile showcasing a set of dimples that probably charmed many ladies far and wide. Her gaze traveled lower to his wide shoulders and broad chest, and when her eyes continued their perusal to inspect his—

"Margaret." Reese interrupted her scrutiny.

Maggie raised her chin and stared at her brother as if she had done nothing wrong. "Yes?"

"Graham introduced his new assistant, and you never responded." He nodded for her to rise.

Maggie sighed softly enough that no one heard her, or so she thought. "I apologize for my wandering thoughts."

Her mother shook her head in disappointment while Graham snickered at the silent reprimand. The look Evelyn and Reese exchanged confused her. However, it was the stranger's response that awoke Maggie from her disenchanted view of proper decorum.

He stepped forward and murmured low enough for only Maggie's ears, "Proper behavior is always a bore when one would rather just truly be themselves." Then his voice rose for everyone to hear. "It is a pleasure to meet you, Lady Margaret."

Maggie stared at him in a daze. His comment spoke the truth of her viewpoint on the subject. Why couldn't it be so simple? Why must one pretend to be someone they are not? Her mind wandered again as she contemplated his comment, and she forgot to acknowledge him again.

"Margaret Ann," her mother hissed.

Maggie swung her gaze to the gentleman to find his amused smile beaming down at her. He was extremely tall. "The pleasure is all mine . . ." Maggie paused, unable to finish since she had missed how she should address him.

"Lord Dracott," Graham spoke in a dramatic stage whisper.

Maggie rolled her eyes at Graham. "Lord Dracott, I hope you enjoy your visit."

He nodded. "I hope one day I might. For now, my visit is only for overnight before I return to London."

"You are not staying long?" Maggie shifted her attention back to Graham.

Graham shrugged. "'Fraid not."

Lord Dracott forgotten, Maggie pouted over losing her only ally. But after Graham's comments when he arrived, she realized she had lost her last chance to navigate her way out of the season. It would appear she must endure the drudgery the ton would surely provide for her amusement. If she had to spend the next few months wearing a polite smile through many torturous dances, picnics, soirees, musicals, and countless balls, then she would enjoy her remaining days outdoors. And she would enjoy those moments now.

"Mother, may I retire to my room to write a letter for Graham to deliver to Eden?"

"You may." Her mother granted Maggie permission to leave.

Maggie rushed to her bedchamber to change. After she slammed the door, she discarded each piece of her attire into piles spread about the room. Then she dug into the wardrobe and pulled out a pair of breeches and one of Graham's old lawn shirts. After she yanked on her boots and tied her hair on top of her head with a hat pulled over the long tresses, she snuck down the servant's staircase. She closed her eyes, breathed in the fresh air, and let the warm sunshine wash away the dread of her future days to come.

On her way to the stables, she stopped to admire the beauty surrounding her. The green fields sprinkled with wildflowers beckoned her to enjoy what time she had left. Maggie took off in a sprint to reach the stables and saddle Penelope. Without taking a single glance back at Worthington Hall, Maggie rode off to catch every ray of sunshine the day held.

Crispin Dracott watched Lady Margaret and her magnificent steed ride away. The lady was an enchanting creature he wished to become better acquainted with. But if he allowed himself that pleasure, it would jeopardize what he had worked for this past year.

With each day, he drew closer to losing the shackles that kept him locked in a prison of his own demise, one he had been too young to understand when forced into the illicit underworld of money and danger. Recently, greed and destruction had awakened him into wanting a better life for himself. After he finished this last assignment, he would be free to live his remaining days repenting for his crimes.

The last thing he needed was a spoiled debutante distracting him. Even one as amusing as Margaret Worthington—or Maggie, as her family called her. She fit the name perfectly. Young and carefree without a worry in the world, a position he had never had the fortune to experience. However, he wondered how it would feel if he allowed himself to indulge in the fantasy.

But he didn't have the luxury of indulging in the beauty. Nor would Graham Worthington allow him anywhere near his sister. The gentleman may find amusement in Maggie's antics, but beneath all the teasing, Worth would be a fierce protector of his sister's innocence. In truth, Dracott didn't want Maggie to lose any of her naivety because of his influence, no matter how tempting of a package she may be.

And she was very tempting indeed. With her dark, luxurious hair hanging down her back in curls. Curves she probably didn't fully appreciate yet. And the most gorgeous backside he had ever seen. Her arse molded into her saddle as her thighs gripped the horse's flanks. Dracott broke out into a sweat imagining Maggie straddling him.

As for the rest of her body, the dress she had worn earlier was too prim and proper for him to know what other delights her body held. And the lawn shirt she wore now hung on her body, hiding her curves, much to his disappointment.

Evelyn Worthington spoke next to him. "I hope you do not think too unkindly of my sister-in-law. She is reluctant to begin her first season. If you cannot tell, she enjoys horses more than polite company."

Dracott dragged his gaze away from the window and focused on the lady before him. He hoped he didn't draw attention to his interest in Maggie. "I have no unkind opinion of the lady. In fact, I only envy her ability to not allow society to dictate her actions."

Evelyn laughed. "I will admit we try to rein them in from time to time. But Maggie has a spirit that cannot be contained."

Dracott glanced back outside, even though the topic of their conversation had ridden out of his view. "Well, for her sake, I hope Lady Margaret is allowed to keep her spirit alive. For she will need it once she makes her debut."

After he made his comment, Lady Worthington pinched her lips and scrutinized him, and he feared he had revealed his interest. However, she soon graced him with a smile again. "I hope so too."

Dracott breathed a sigh of relief when young Mina started fussing on her father's lap. The earl stood with the toddler, murmuring in her ear. Lady Worthington rushed to their side and rubbed her hand along the child's back. The earl smiled fondly at his wife, and the countess blushed a lovely shade of pink.

Dracott's gaze traveled around the parlor to see how Worth and his mother reacted to the intimate exchange. Smiles rested on their faces as they watched the small family. However, Dracott realized that even though his boss and his mother stood outside of the exchange, they were part of the affection shared. Even with a stranger in the room, they displayed nothing but genuine fondness. This family was a novelty he had never witnessed before.

He was always one to adapt to his environment and could easily implement himself into this family and belong. However, if he thought Maggie was a temptation to avoid, a warm and caring family was the ultimate risk he must stay away from. Because they were the picture of what his dreams represented for himself, dreams that would never become a reality.

No matter how much he wished otherwise.

Chapter Two

THE DOOR TO THE outer office slammed shut with enough force for the gentlemen gathered around the table to halt their discussion. They shuffled the papers they examined out of sight into a drawer and each of them took a seat at their own desk and pretended interest in their individual paperwork.

Reese Worthington strode into his brother's detective agency with purpose and pointed a finger at Worth. "I am finished. She is yours to deal with for the season."

Worth chuckled. "What has she done now?"

Worthington threw his hat on the desk and ran his hand through his hair in frustration. "The correct question is what has Maggie not done the past two months since we arrived in London."

Barrett Ralston, Graham Worthington's business partner, chuckled. "Gemma told me over breakfast this morning how Maggie asked Lady Burrows during her luncheon when she was due to give birth and then continued to describe how a mare gave birth."

Worth frowned. "I did not know Lady Burrows was expecting."

Worthington growled. "She is not with child."

Dracott tried to hold in his snicker but failed, which only infuriated the earl and earned him a glare. "My apologies."

Worth stood and urged his brother into a chair. "Stop trying to intimidate my assistant." He nodded at Ralston to pour his brother a drink.

Once he calmed his nerves, Worthington made his demands. "You are to escort Mother and Maggie to the Sinclair Ball this evening. Not only are you to escort Maggie, but you must never leave her side. Under no circumstances is she not to be within your eyesight. If she accepts a gentleman's offer to dance, you are to watch her from the sidelines. However, it is doubtful she will since she has refused every offer since our arrival in town. Then you must question why she accepted the dance because it is her way of escaping your clutches. I will admit this only once and I will deny it if anyone ever repeats it. The conniving minx has outwitted me on more than one occasion."

Ralston shook his head. "I sympathize with you. However, Maggie's antics are hilarious and I enjoy hearing about them."

Worthington scoffed. "Just wait until your sisters make their debut. From what I hear, they are a handful in their own rights."

Ralston sobered. "Ah, damn."

Worthington took another gulp of his drink. "Exactly."

"I cannot escort them this evening. We had a break in a case, and I am needed elsewhere," Worth interjected.

Worthington leaned back in the chair with a confident smile and crossed a leg over his knee. "I knew you would find an excuse. So I will only mention one name that will make you understand my demand clearly."

"You wouldn't dare," Worth snarled.

Dracott's gaze flipped back and forth between the brothers. Who held the power to sway his boss into abandoning his plans for the evening? He slid forward in his seat, eager to hear.

"Eden," Worthington answered with the dare.

The office grew silent when Worthington declared the name of the lady who held the strings in their investigation. If Worth pulled Eden from her latest assignment, then the plans they had put in place would have been for naught. Even now she held a pivotal position, and they couldn't afford to replace her with anyone else.

Worthington continued with his threat. "I have allowed Eden to amuse herself by playing detective with you because she enjoys the thrill and it hasn't tarnished her reputation. So much that I have even covered her absence with Mother when needed. However, if you recall the promise you made that if I needed your help, you would make yourself available or else Eden must partake in the season to find a husband."

Silence settled over the office while Worth and Ralston weighed their options. If Worth didn't escort the ladies this evening, they would lose Eden. She was their eyes and ears at all the functions, finding out information none of them could gain elsewhere. Dracott had only met Eden Worthington a few times, but he admired her fierce determination to the cause. However, if Worth attended the ball, then they must wait before they implemented the next stage in capturing the leader of the thievery ring tormenting England.

Dracott noticed the slight signal Ralston gave Worth. To most people, it was a twitch, but to the trained eye, it spoke of something far more valuable. An unspoken message explaining the understanding between partners.

"Very well," Worth answered his brother.

Worthington rose. "I thought you would see reason."

Worth growled. "You did not leave me much choice."

"I am curious about one aspect of your hesitation." Worthington strolled to the door, and Worth waited for his brother to comment, not bothering to ask what stoked his curiosity. Worthington turned, keeping his hand on the doorknob. "What case is Eden involved with that you cannot release her from?"

Dracott frowned when Worth and Ralston both avoided Worthington's stare. Ever since Dracott joined the organization a few months ago, Worthington had stopped by on occasion and they had discussed their cases openly, even seeking his advice on how to proceed with them. It was on the tip of his tongue to mention the intel they had received about an old case. But Ralston shot him a warning to stay silent. So Dracott dropped his head and pretended a renewed interest in the paperwork spread across his desk.

"A recent case that I do not wish for her to blow her cover on. It involves a missing necklace," Worth explained.

Worthington nodded. "The ladies will be ready at eight o'clock. Oh, and bring your assistant."

Worth frowned. "Why?"

"Because Evelyn is under the impression that he holds a calming influence over Maggie," Worthington explained before strolling out the door.

Worth scowled after his brother. "Damn him."

Ralston sighed. "Another distraction placed in our path."

"Sorry, mate." Worth poured himself a drink. "We must postpone our plan for another evening."

"We wouldn't have found success anyhow. Without Falcone's information, we are at a standstill. Once he arrives, we can secure the ringleader's capture," Ralston stated.

"Can you please explain why you didn't inform your brother of the information we received on the old case?" Dracott asked.

Ralston tried to make Worth see reason. "You need to tell him, Worth. Once he learns of her return, this will affect him and Evelyn. Because the lady will exact her revenge against your brother and his wife. Rumor is that she holds onto her bitterness at Worthington for throwing her over for Evelyn."

"Because I plan to destroy Lady Langdale before she even steps foot in London," Worth declared.

Despite his declaration, they were already too late to make the threat happen.

Maggie rolled her eyes. If she had to listen to her sister Noel describe how *divine* her fiancé was any longer, she would lose the contents of her stomach. Then her mother would discipline her on how a lady never showed any sign of illness in front of others under any circumstance. But she had grown tired of the endless praises Noel directed for Lord Ravencroft. Or Gregory, as Noel gloated in more intimate company. Either way, Maggie no longer wished to listen to another word.

When Noel flashed her ring again to her many admirers, Maggie slipped away while she had a chance. Graham had dropped Maggie in Noel's clutches and sauntered away to the card room. Excitement had coursed through her when Graham arrived to escort them to the Sinclair Ball. Reese and Evelyn had spent the evening at home since Evelyn didn't feel well. Maggie suspected they would announce the impending arrival of a new family member soon. However, Graham had refused to allow Maggie to join him in the card room. She had thought Eden would help relieve the boredom, but her sister had yet to arrive.

Which left Maggie at the mercy of hearing Noel gush over Ravenscroft's proposal for the umpteenth time.

It wasn't as if she didn't hold joy for her sister's happiness. She did. Or she would if it were a different gentleman. However, Lord Ravencroft drew out Maggie's dislike of his suspicious activities. He may present himself as a doting fiancé by showering Noel with many gifts, but Maggie questioned his behavior. When no one paid him any attention, Maggie noticed a permanent frown on his face. Especially after interacting with Noel.

Shouldn't a gentleman who acted as he did with Noel always express happiness, even when he was apart from her? Each couple she was familiar with, the gentleman walked in a state of marital bliss, even when he was apart from his wife. Reese was a perfect example after he married Evelyn. He never let a day pass without expressing his happiness to everyone around him. Maggie hoped to find a gentleman who showed her the same devotion.

She slipped outside onto the dark balcony and glanced over her shoulder. Once she saw no one followed her, she continued down the stairs and into the garden. She understood the risk if someone caught her and promised herself she would be quick. She only wanted to take a peek at Sinclair's new mare. Maggie had overheard Jasper Sinclair discussing the horse with Reese earlier in the week, and she wanted to see the beauty.

She pulled off her slippers and hitched her skirts above her knees before she reached the stables. Since the stable hands had to take care of the carriages arriving for the ball, the stables sat empty, much to her advantage. She wandered up and down the aisles until she came upon the golden-haired beauty. Maggie dropped her skirts and climbed up a rail to peer into the stall. The foal slept next to her mama. She sighed, wishing to stroke the soft mane, but she didn't wish to disturb them.

Dracott followed Maggie once she slipped away from the ballroom. Worth had given him explicit orders concerning his sister. Dracott was to remain hidden during the ball and watch the beauty every second. If she wandered away, he was to follow and keep her out of trouble. Worth didn't care if Maggie took part in the ball or not. He only cared if his sister didn't give anyone reason to gossip about her behavior.

Worth sympathized with his sister and didn't wish to play the villain. The other members of the Worthington family already applied enough pressure on Maggie's entrance into society. Worth didn't wish to add to it.

When Maggie ventured through the gardens and continued to the mews, Dracott realized her destination. He shook his head once she bent over to take off her slippers. At least she had the decency to raise her skirts before she ventured into the stables. He picked up his pace. If anyone was to catch her unescorted, who knew what would happen? She risked her virtue for a mere glimpse at a horse.

He soon learned how much trouble Margaret Worthington actually was.

He found her crouched over the railing, reaching out to stroke the mare's coat. When she lost her grip and tumbled over, losing his position flashed through his mind. Dracott lurched forward and grabbed Maggie before she landed face-first in the hay. He drew her back against his chest, breathing a sigh of relief.

However, the spitfire in his arms reacted differently. She thrashed around and kicked at his legs. When her head flew back and smashed him in the nose, he dropped her.

"Bloody settle down. I only tried to save you from falling!" Dracott shouted.

Maggie winced at the order coming from the gentleman who had haunted her dreams of late. Lord Dracott stood above her, scowling at her while he clenched his nose. She scrambled to her feet and urged his hands away from his face. Then she brushed her fingers across the redness.

"I apologize, my lord. I thought you were accosting me," Maggie explained.

"You are lucky that wasn't my intention. You act irresponsibly by wandering around without a chaperone to see to your welfare," Dracott reprimanded her. "You would have been helpless if someone disreputable came along and took advantage of you."

Dracott struggled to keep a stern voice with Maggie's hand caressing his face. Her gentle touch undid him. His fingers rolled into a fist to keep from drawing her into his arms and kissing her. Her wide eyes and pouty lips were a temptation he struggled to resist. Why did his assignment this evening have to involve her? Ever since he met the debutante, she had consumed his thoughts. Any time someone mentioned her name, his ears perked to hear about her latest escapades.

Maggie's lips quivered at his anger. No one had ever expressed such fury at her before. Whenever she got into mischief in the past, her family would explain what she did wrong and then laugh about it later. She didn't know how to respond to Lord Dracott's reaction. For the first time in her life, she stayed silent. Perhaps if she never responded to him, he would calm down and escort her back inside before her family learned of her disappearance. Shoot. They would learn anyway since it was Graham's assistant who had found her wandering alone.

"Do you not understand?" Dracott bellowed.

Darn. Her mind had wandered again. What was it about Lord Dracott that always distracted her? However, his question was easy enough to answer. "Yes. I understand, my lord."

Dracott narrowed his eyes at the young miss. He recognized the dazed expression to know that he didn't hold her attention during his rant. Perhaps if he showed her what might happen to her, she would think twice before sneaking away again.

He dragged her to him, pressing her arms to her side in his clutch. Her head jerked up, and she stared at him in surprise. When she didn't resist his embrace, he pressed her tighter against him. With one arm wrapped around her waist, he used his other hand to caress her, starting with a brush of his fingers across her cheek. Then he traced a path along her neck and settled against the curve of her breast. Dracott felt the hitch of Maggie's breath deep in his soul. His body warned him to cease his attempt to teach her a lesson, but he ignored the warnings and continued the sweet torment.

Maggie struggled to catch her breath. She didn't understand Lord Dracott's intentions, nor did she care. Was this passion? While she should question him, she also longed to see where this might lead. Did he intend to kiss her? Her eyelids drifted down as she waited in anticipation. While she never wished to have her first kiss in the stables, she didn't care as long as he placed his lips upon hers soon.

Maggie's lips opened enough for her to run the tip of her tongue across to wet them. Her body tingled in anticipation for his mouth to press against hers when his warm breath tickled against her cheek. Her fantasies of late were about to come true. When Dracott growled, she knew he was about to fulfill them.

However, instead of kissing her, he dropped his hold and strode away. Maggie's eyes flew open, and she grabbed at the railing to steady her trembling limbs.

Soon he was upon her again with his hands fisted at his hips. Instead of shame washing over Maggie, a rush of desire settled between them. And she watched Lord Dracott fight against the attraction. With each ragged breath he drew in, Maggie realized he had attempted to teach her a lesson but failed. Was it because he found her desirable? Or did he realize he had overstepped his bounds by placing his hands on her person? If either of her brothers learned of his impropriety, he would be a dead man.

With a smile, she picked up the slippers she had dropped and sauntered out of the stables, confident that Dracott would keep her brief visit to the stables a secret. Well, at least for now. She glanced over her shoulder at him and saw how he followed her at a discreet distance. She bent over, slid on her slippers, and then skipped her way through the garden.

What in the hell had he done? He had almost kissed her. At least he had come to his senses and stopped himself before he made a horrible mistake. While attempting to show Maggie what might happen if a gentleman came upon her with dubious intentions, he'd almost committed the very act of ruining her.

Now he couldn't give Worth a detailed report of her activity without implicating himself. Because if he told of Maggie's adventure to the stables, then she would spill the truth of their encounter. The devious minx had him right where she wanted him. He would ruin everything he had worked to achieve and risk his position if he told on her. Also, Maggie Worthington had proven this evening how much of a temptation she was and how he must avoid her at all costs.

No matter how alluring she might be.

Chapter Three

M AGGIE SLIPPED BACK INSIDE undetected. However, before she located her family, familiar hands drew her onto the ballroom floor amongst the other dancers. She wanted to question Lord Dracott about his intention, but she grew light-headed when he twirled her around in a circle. Not from the dance, but from his touch. She thought she had outwitted him, but he seemed to attack her senses from all angles with each twist and turn of the dance. Once the music ended, he bowed, and she followed his lead with a curtsy. Then he held out his arm for her to take.

"Follow my lead if you wish to keep your family's questions at bay," Dracott muttered near her ear.

Maggie nodded. "I thought . . ."

Dracott gave her an arrogant smile. "Your first mistake."

Maggie lifted her eyebrows. "And my second?"

He chuckled. "Ahh, a mistake I will not reveal to keep you at a disadvantage."

Before Maggie responded, Dracott escorted her back to the bosom of her family. Noel stood gazing at Lord Ravencroft adoringly. Her mother and Graham appeared deep in conversation, and Eden arched her eyebrow at Maggie's companion. Once her mother saw her, she stopped talking and glanced around to see if anyone paid them any attention.

"Where have you been?" Lady Worthington hissed.

"I told you, Mama, Maggie retired to the refreshment room for a spell," Eden interrupted.

"It appears Lord Dracott and Maggie were sharing a dance." Worth slapped Dracott on the back. "Wherever you found her, thank you for returning her safely," he whispered in Dracott's ear, his relief more than clear.

"I apologize for any misunderstanding. I noticed Lady Margaret looking for her family, and since it was time for our dance she agreed to, I saw no harm in joining the set," Dracott explained.

"Hmph." Lady Worthington narrowed her gaze on the couple. Her daughter still clutched the lord's arm.

Lady Worthington wasn't blind to how her daughter's eyes danced with stars, nor the favored glances Lord Dracott paid her daughter. If it weren't for Graham's praise for his new assistant, she would worry. Lord Dracott had done nothing to prove himself otherwise. He worked tirelessly with Graham to bring justice to victimized individuals, so she held nothing but the utmost respect for the gentleman. However, she wished for Maggie to enjoy her first season and not fall for the first gentleman who paid her attention. She cleared her throat, staring at Maggie's hand resting on Lord Dracott's sleeve.

Lord Dracott, too captivated by Maggie's spell, still held onto her hand. Lady Worthington's subtle message finally caught his attention. He released Maggie's arm and stepped off to the side. "Thank you for the dance, Lady Margaret."

Maggie frowned at the loss of Lord Dracott's touch but realized her family stared at her differently with their own queries of interest. "It was my pleasure, Lord Dracott."

"Oh, Lord Dracott, I am happy you have attended this ball," Noel gushed. "I have been singing your praises to my fiancé about how much you have helped Graham this past year and now you two can meet. Allow me to introduce you to Lord Ravencroft."

Dracott hoped his expression and Ravencroft's remained impartial after the introduction. Although he knew the gentleman Lady Noel was engaged to, he never thought they would cross paths this soon. While he feared he would give himself away, he worried Ravencroft wouldn't be able to control his fury at Dracott's arrival in London. When Ravencroft never contacted him, he had made a rash decision to infiltrate the investigation himself instead of waiting for Ravenscroft's word of a safe return.

"Lord Dracott, I have heard nothing but praise for your insightful investigative skills." Lord Ravencroft shook Dracott's hand, applying enough pressure to make him grimace.

Dracott returned the rough handshake, applying his own pressure. "Thank you. And may I offer my congratulations on your upcoming nuptials? You must be very proud to make such a conquest, Lord Ravencroft."

"I am but a humble servant to my adoring bride-to-be." Ravencroft lifted Noel's hand and placed a kiss across her knuckles.

Dracott plastered on a smile and turned toward the rest of the Worthington family. "Ladies. Gentlemen. I hope you enjoy the rest of your evening."

They each expressed their sentiments, and Dracott left their side. He walked through the ballroom, blending in with the crowd. Once again he encased himself in the shadows to guard the one lady who made him lose all common sense. He hoped he had convinced Worth and Lady Worthington

of their absence. If not, then he would have to find a new
position.

Eden smirked. "He is most handsome."

"Mmm, yes," Maggie murmured as she watched Dracott
stroll away.

"Or, as Noel would describe, most divine," Eden teased.

"Mmm, yes," Maggie repeated.

"Oh, dear. It is as I feared." Eden snapped her fingers in front
of Maggie's face.

Maggie startled out of her daze. "What do you fear?"

Eden's smile held a secret she wasn't ready to reveal.
"Nothing, my dear. How was your dance with Lord Dracott?"

"Heavenly." Maggie sighed, searching for Lord Dracott. But
she had lost him in the crowd.

Eden laughed but said no more. If she wasn't mistaken, her
younger sister had fallen smitten with Lord Dracott's charm.
She knew Mama's intention was only for Maggie to become
accustomed to society in her first season. Not to make a
match so early. But the heart wants what the heart wants. And
Maggie's heart wanted Lord Dracott. She only hoped Lord
Dracott wanted Maggie in the same regard.

Dracott tugged at his cravat until it came undone. Then he
ripped it off and tossed it across the bed. The evening had
frustrated him, causing him to feel a restless energy that, if
he didn't contain it, would end in disaster. In the past, when
he couldn't control his emotions, his behavior had turned
reckless, and at this moment in his life, he didn't dare act upon
his frustrations.

A simple miss set him on edge. Her penance for landing
herself in trouble now involved him as a guilty party. Not to

mention her delectable lips he wished to devour. At least he had come to his senses before he ravished her. Because if he had, he wouldn't have stopped. He would have pulled one kiss after another from her lips.

"Damn," he muttered. He must stop fantasizing about a lady out of his reach.

He lit a candle to see his way around the small room. It was a pathetic living area, but he paid for it honestly, something he hadn't been able to do in the past. If his employers or their families saw his meager residence, it would draw forth too many questions. He couldn't answer them without telling more lies. So to fool them, he made sure he wore the finest clothing and ate at well-known dining establishments so they couldn't question him. Hell. It was bad enough he lied about his standing in society.

"*Lord Dracott*. How are you, little brother?" a voice drawled from the darkened corner.

Dracott jumped and dropped the candle. He stomped on the small flame until he snuffed it out. "Damn you!"

"Is that any way to greet your *brother*?"

Dracott relit the candle, holding it up to see Ravencroft lounging in his only chair. The infuriating gentleman had also confiscated his only bottle of gin. Dracott noted he had drunk half the bottle. This meeting wouldn't go smoothly.

"Why are you here?"

Ravencroft took a drink. "I think that is my question *for you*."

Dracott swiped the bottle away and set it back on the shelf. "Since I never heard from you for over a year, I struck out on my own."

"That was because I was laying the groundwork for our plan," Ravencroft snarled.

"Never in our plans was the agenda of engaging yourself to a Worthington chit."

Ravencroft stretched out his legs. "She was too tempting to resist. You must understand because my eyes didn't deceive me this evening. You have become quite smitten with my fiancée's sister."

Dracott growled. "Nonsense."

Ravencroft tsked. "It never sets well when one denies something so fiercely."

"Since you have deviated from our original plan, what are you hoping to achieve by tying yourself to Noel Worthington for an eternity?" Dracott asked.

"I am hoping for many lively evenings and a fat purse once I say I do." Ravencroft waggled his eyebrows.

Dracott growled. "Stop with your crude behavior. It is beneath you."

"Oh, the street urchin has turned all proper," Ravencroft mocked him.

Dracott advanced on Ravencroft with his fist pulled back. Before Dracott took a step farther, Ravencroft shot from the chair and shoved Dracott back. His feet tangled in the rug, and he landed on the bed with Ravencroft towering over him with a scowl. He cowered at his brother's fury. Even though he knew Ravencroft would never harm him, it didn't stop his instinct to tremble and for fear to kick in.

"Damn," Ravencroft muttered, backing away from the bed.

Once Dracott gathered himself under control, he accepted the hand held out to him. He grabbed the bottle off the shelf and took a long swig. The gin burned its way down to his gut, shaking off the fear.

"Sorry, mate. I didn't realize you still suffered from the same terrors."

Dracott set the bottle back, noticing how his hand still shook. "Only when I am stressed do they flare to life."

Ravencroft sighed. "Why couldn't you have waited? I am so close to finishing this last job."

"Lady L paid a visit to your estate six months ago, adding a twist to our freedom."

Ravencroft gritted his teeth. "Damn her. What does she want now?"

"She heard of Lady Margaret's debut and wants to make the ball her mark."

Ravencroft tightened his hands into fists. "Why must she continue to make our life difficult?"

"Because our mother revolted against her and she seeks her revenge against us to pay for our mother's sins."

"That does not explain why you are working for Graham Worthington and Barrett Ralston. Do you understand the risk you take if they ever discover your ties to Lady L?"

Dracott arched an eyebrow. "No more of a risk you take engaging yourself to Lady Noel."

"Mine is more believable than yours. I actually hold a title and have an estate. It might need repairs and my coffers are empty, but once we speak our vows, I will gain a sizable dowry and my reputation as a dissolute earl will be remedied. Not to mention I will have the power of her brother, the earl, at my disposal to squash any rumors."

"You are an earl in your own right," Dracott argued.

"But a penniless one that holds no credit. Whereas you are impersonating a viscount who holds no reputable title."

"My father was a gentleman."

"But your mother was a whore," Ravencroft snarled.

"Who was also your mother too," Dracott reminded him.

"Yes, a stunning countess in her day who my father worshipped. But his devotion was never enough for her, and she always wanted more. She spread her thighs for whoever paid her attention until she caught herself pregnant with another man's bastard."

Dracott clutched at his heart. "Your brotherly love holds strong."

Ravencroft fumed. "As a result, our mother wreaked havoc on both of our lives with her foolish acts of betrayal to anyone who crossed her path. Now, when we are so close to paying off her final debt, the future I carved out for myself hangs in jeopardy."

"Was I even a part of your future?"

Ravencroft blew out a breath. "Yes. Only now we must revise our plan to accommodate the thorn in our side. I wish you would have stayed at the estate."

Dracott winced. "Sorry. When you never sent word, I . . ."

Ravencroft nodded. "I understand. You thought I had abandoned you as everyone else in your life had and you lost your trust in me. Now tell me what your role is with Worth and Ralston."

"I assist them with their cases."

"Are they investigating the new rash of robberies?"

Dracott couldn't meet his brother's eyes without giving his role away. "We caught word about them, but they haven't contacted us to assist with them."

"We must find a way for the Runners to ask for your agency's help."

"It is too dangerous," Dracott warned.

Ravencroft rubbed the back of his neck. "Let me mull this over to find us a solution. I will send word to meet in a few days."

Dracott watched his brother blow out the candles and slip out the door without a sound. Ravencroft had once held the promise of a prominent role in society, only to fall victim to their mother's manipulations. Once his father passed away, he had gone in search of the mother who had abandoned him only to find her deep in a thievery ring that she pulled him into, where Ravencroft met a brother he never knew he had.

Dracott had been fourteen when he first met Ravencroft. By then, he had spent a lifetime at the abuse of his mother and the other culprits involved in the thievery ring. They would use him as a pawn in their escapades, causing him to be their beating pole while they made away with stolen goods.

Dracott shuddered at the memories. Whenever someone advanced on him in violence, it would trigger those memories to resurface, leaving him trembling like a coward. His brother was correct. What had he gotten himself into? So far, the cases he had assisted on were mild indiscretions. His involvement to help capture Lady L could lead him to freeze on the spot instead of assisting.

However, it was too late to withdraw.

Maggie's hand trailed along the railing as she hurried down the staircase. She hoped to catch Graham and Lord Dracott before they left for the morning. In her younger days, she would have hopped on the banister and slid down, reaching the bottom faster. But she wished for Lord Dracott to view her as a mature lady, not as the hoyden everyone referred to her as.

She had missed them the past three mornings since she was out with Reese on their morning rides through Hyde Park. But Reese had an early morning appointment and couldn't ride today, which left her able to spend a little extra time on her appearance. Once she reached the bottom step, she smoothed her hands along her skirts and patted her hair, assuring herself that she was presentable.

Maggie scowled when she noticed Lord Ravencroft holding court, amusing her mother and sisters with some far-fetched tale as she strolled into the breakfast room. Graham and Lord Dracott were deep in discussion, paying her no attention on her arrival. The old Maggie would have flounced into breakfast, crying over another boring luncheon she must attend. However, today she would act differently. She would attempt to act like a lady by sipping her tea and nibbling on a scone, even though she longed for a slab of bacon and eggs.

Maggie slid a plain scone onto her plate and sat down next to Lord Dracott. After the servant poured her tea, she added sugar and honey, letting it cool before she attempted a drink. She cut the scone the way her mother did and took a small bite. Her stomach rumbled in protest at the meager offering. She pressed a hand over her stomach, hoping no one had overheard.

"Here, Mags, take my bacon." Graham leaned over Dracott to toss the strips onto her plate. "No need to go hungry. We have plenty."

Maggie blushed a fiery red. She closed her eyes, counting until she reached a level of patience to deal with her brother. She should have known her family wouldn't allow her to make a memorable presentation toward Lord Dracott. They would forever see her as Mags, the uncontrollable sibling they tormented with their teasing.

Maggie pasted on a smile. "Thank you, Graham."

Maggie took a bite of the bacon. She knew not to cause a spectacle because it would only prompt more teasing. Her brother appeared satisfied and continued his conversation with Dracott, while Maggie sat in morbid embarrassment that her stomach had rumbled loudly enough for the gentleman she tried to impress to have heard.

The end of the table erupted in laughter, with her mother gushing over Lord Ravencroft. Maggie glared at the earl. She understood how Noel had fallen for his pretentious charm. But Eden and her mother, too? She thought they were wiser. Didn't they see through his false charm to understand the man he truly was? A man she needed to reveal before Noel spoke her wedding vows to him and became stuck in a miserable marriage.

"One would think you dislike Lord Ravencroft," Dracott whispered.

"Because I do," Maggie stated.

"May I inquire as to why?"

Maggie narrowed her gaze, contemplating if she could trust him. However, if she told him and he betrayed her, then Lord Dracott wasn't the gentleman she thought he was.

She frowned. "I am not sure yet. I cannot shake this sense that he hides something and his intentions are not honorable where Noel is concerned."

Dracott took a sip of tea, trying to hide his reaction to Maggie's opinion of Ravencroft. "Your concerns are understandable. The sisterly bond you hold with Lady Noel only wishes for her happiness with her marriage. And for you to guarantee her happiness, you must hold satisfaction that she made the right choice with Lord Ravencroft."

Maggie looked surprised that he understood her. "Yes, exactly."

Dracott nodded at the earl. "Perhaps if you spent more time in his company, you might see how genuine his intentions are."

Maggie scoffed. "More than a minute alone with him tells me enough."

"If I were to look into his activities, would that help to ease your mind?" Dracott asked.

"You would do that for me?"

"Yes," Dracott answered.

He would do anything for Maggie. He walked a dangerous line by agreeing to look into Ravencroft. He didn't need to watch his brother to understand his true character. Dracott held firsthand knowledge of how his brother went to any lengths to protect the people he cared for. While he didn't agree on the basis of Ravencroft's engagement to Lady Noel, his brother would see to the lady's happiness to the best of his capability. Now he only needed to convince Maggie of Ravencroft's honorable intentions before she discovered his more dishonorable ones.

"Are you ready, Dracott? I told Ralston we would arrive at the office by ten o'clock," Graham asked.

Dracott nodded. "Thank you, Lady Worthington, for another pleasant breakfast."

Lady Worthington smiled kindly at him. "You're welcome. We enjoy your company."

Dracott stood and slid his chair underneath the table. "A pleasure, as always, Lady Margaret."

Maggie smiled at him.

"Do you gentleman mind if I join you? I have an appointment nearby your office," Ravencroft asked.

"Not at all," Graham answered.

Dracott stood behind Maggie, waiting for Ravencroft to say his farewells. He was close enough to sweep his fingers across the back of her neck. To rest his hand on her shoulder. To bend his head and whisper the goodbye he wanted to express, one held with promises of how he would kiss her when they met later. So many promises he ached to share with her.

Maggie felt the warmth of Dracott against her back. She imagined his eyes caressing her. Did he ache to kiss her as much as she ached for his lips to possess her? She wished they were alone. Maggie wanted to hug him to show her gratitude for his offer to help with her suspicions. And if the hug happened to turn into a kiss? Well, she would have no complaint with that.

When a set of hands rested on her shoulders and a head bent to whisper in her ear, her eyes widened and she stiffened. Dracott wouldn't act so boldly to touch her in front of her family. Would he?

"A pleasure? The poor bloke doesn't know you quite well yet. Does he, Mags?" Graham teased.

Maggie swatted at him. "I thought you had to leave."

Graham chuckled. "I will miss you too."

Maggie rolled her eyes. After the gentlemen left, she rose and prepared herself a plate worthy of eating. When she returned to the table, she found three sets of eyes focused on her, watching her with amusement.

"What?" Maggie growled.

"Nothing, my dear. Did you enjoy your conversation with Lord Dracott?" Lady Worthington asked.

"Mmm," Maggie answered, filling her mouth with eggs.

"She appears quite taken with him," Eden commented.

"Who is Maggie taken with?" Evelyn asked, strolling into the breakfast room with Mina on her hip.

"Lord Dracott," Noel said.

Evelyn sat down, settling Mina on her lap. "I believe he is taken with her, too."

Maggie stilled, taking in Evelyn's comment. Was he? She didn't dare ponder this new information in front of them. She sensed their gazes centered on her, so she continued eating, never once joining the conversation. Her feelings for Lord Dracott were too new, and she didn't wish to share how he made her feel yet. If ever.

"He presents himself as a nice enough gentleman. What is Reese's opinion of Lord Dracott?" Mama asked Evelyn.

"He is undecided. While he wishes for Maggie to find a more established gentleman, he wouldn't stand in their way if Lord Dracott is her choice."

"Mmm," Mama murmured, scrutinizing Maggie. "We shall continue with the debut and socializing. Lord Dracott has yet to express his intentions, and until he does, we must give Maggie every opportunity to meet other gentlemen."

Noel voiced her opinion. "Lord Dracott is very handsome. Not quite as divine as Ravencroft, but he is perfect for Maggie."

Eden gasped. "Not quite as divine as Ravencroft? Then he will not do at all."

Everyone but Noel burst into laughter. But when Mina quoted Eden with "Not at all," Noel joined in. Ever since Noel's first season, she had rated every gentleman as divine. However, only Ravencroft held the title of the most divine. Maggie must reward her niece for distracting her mother to stop discussing her future. She may find Lord Dracott interesting, but it didn't mean she wanted to spend the rest of her life with him.

"Can I take Mina to the park?" Maggie asked Evelyn.

Evelyn wiped jelly off Mina's cheek. "What do you say, poppet? Would you like to visit the park with Maggie?"

Mina clapped her hands. "Yay. Yay. Park."

Maggie gathered Mina and carried her upstairs for a coat and bonnet. She hoped a bit of fresh air would help clear the foolish thoughts floating through her head. Her family's opinion of Lord Dracott's interest only gave Maggie hope.

But was it a foolish hope?

Chapter Four

ANOTHER WEEK PASSED WITH Maggie attending more balls than she wanted to remember. Sometimes two or three in one evening. And at each ball she stood on the sidelines, refusing one offer to dance after another. She didn't understand why she drew so much attention. But during the dances her mother forced her to accept, each gentleman would rave about her beauty, gracefulness, and how she possessed an agreeable smile. One gentleman called the teeth in her mouth a sign of perfection. The bloke looked her over as if he were buying a piece of horseflesh. Did the gentlemen of the ton choose a bride by how a lady smiled? If so, then she feared who her husband might be. Maggie hoped Reese wouldn't settle her with someone so insensitive as the gentlemen she had met so far.

Then there was the matter of her infatuation with Lord Dracott. The lord consumed her every thought. Any moment she had alone, she fantasized about them together. She dreamed of him kissing her every night. However, whenever their paths crossed, he paid her the utmost respect and never strayed out of character. If anything, he tried to avoid her, and she wondered why. Did he attempt to avoid the promise he had made to confirm Lord Ravencroft's character?

Maggie had done her own investigation but came up empty. Even now, she watched him like a hawk. Lord Ravencroft was the reason she refused any offer to dance because she followed him whenever he left Noel's side. However, on each occasion, he either joined a game of cards or stood on the balcony and smoked a cigar with the other gentlemen. But soon he would slip and she would be there to witness his fall.

"Please keep Maggie within your sight again. Mother said she loses track of her during the balls," Worth told him before sauntering away.

Dracott nodded. By now, he had become accustomed to the order. It wasn't so much of an order but a request, one he accepted without argument because it gave him an excuse to admire Maggie. Worth didn't know how Dracott felt about his sister. And if Worth did, Dracott held no clue on how his employer would react. So he kept his distance, even though he wanted to spend every available second with her. He hoped she would wander away this evening so he could steal a few extra moments with her.

Dracott lifted a drink off a tray and proceeded to the corner. He tipped the glass to his lips when his subject stopped in the middle of the dance and brought her knee up to her dance partner's front. With her swift jab, the bloke dropped to the floor, groaning while Maggie raised her head high and returned to her family. Lady Worthington scolded Maggie but stopped when Maggie explained her actions. The gentlemen in the group laughed while the ladies glared at the assailant. He held no clue what the gentleman did wrong, but by the Worthingtons' reaction, he got what he deserved.

"I taught her that move. I thought she needed to know how to defend herself against an unscrupulous gentleman," Eden commented next to him.

"You taught her well," Dracott murmured, keeping his gaze focused on Maggie.

Eden took a sip of the champagne. "I cannot help but comment on your attention toward Maggie."

Dracott stiffened. "At your brother's request."

"Mmm." Eden kept her gaze focused on the dancers. She didn't need to see Lord Dracott's reaction while they discussed Maggie. She had already seen how he regarded her sister. "Perhaps. But I'm also under the impression you are quite fond of her."

Dracott blew out a breath, unable to deny her observation. The lady was relentless when she wanted information and wouldn't stop until he confessed his infatuation. "Is it too obvious?"

"My family is very observant, and we offer our opinions freely."

"Does Worth know?"

"His thoughts are preoccupied. However, before long he will learn of his own accord. My advice is to mention your interest," Eden offered.

"What if I do not plan to take my interest any further than regarding her from afar?" Dracott asked.

"Then I say you are a fool." Eden clinked her glass with his before she walked away.

Better to be a fool than one who would cause Maggie heartache.

Maggie refused every dance for the remainder of the evening after Lord Gibbings placed his hands on her bottom. He'd thought her loose with her virtue because of her reckless behavior. She knew it would embarrass her family, but she needed to teach him a lesson and any other gentlemen who might hold the opinion that she was free with her affections.

Maggie shifted to the side to get her mother's attention. But Lord Ravencroft snagged her interest instead. He whispered in Noel's ear, and her sister smiled her acceptance of whatever lie he told her. Then he slipped into the crowd. Maggie glanced around and noticed no one paid her any mind.

She snuck away, setting the glass of punch on a nearby table. She caught sight of Ravencroft's burgundy coat and followed him at a discreet distance. When he looked over his shoulder, Maggie ducked and hid behind two gentlemen debating the merits of a bill set before Parliament.

Ravencroft took off again and rounded the corner with Maggie following his trail. When he slipped outside, Maggie followed him into the darkness. He disappeared into a group of trees, and Maggie stopped. She hesitated to follow him any farther. If he caught her, how would she explain herself? But if he didn't, she could see who he met in private.

Maggie gathered her skirts and continued on. She saw a light shining in the distance once she snuck behind a bush. While keeping to the shadows, she advanced closer. Ravencroft was arguing with a hidden figure in a cloak with a hood. She attempted to move closer without revealing herself and settled behind a tree to observe their interaction.

The figure stepped closer to Ravencroft, talking softly enough that Maggie couldn't hear a word they spoke. A hand reached out to brush Ravencroft's hair off his brow, but he grabbed it and held it away from him. The figure struggled, knocking their hood off. Maggie gasped at the lady's long hair blowing in the slight breeze. The lady's cackle pierced the air, causing a shiver to run along Maggie's spine. The evilness of the laughter rocked Maggie to her core. Ravencroft dropped the lady's hand and strode away, putting distance between them. However, Ravencroft grew more agitated as the lady talked. At times he would strike an argument with the lady. However, the lady silenced him by slashing her arm through the air.

Maggie wanted to sneak closer. Whatever they discussed was serious enough that the unflappable Ravencroft appeared out of sorts. Was this lady his mistress? Either way, it proved Maggie was correct to suspect the earl of nefarious activities. She wished Dracott saw what she witnessed for his investigation.

The drama unfolding before Maggie caused her to miss the footsteps sneaking up behind her. When a hand wrapped over her mouth, she attempted to scream, but the firm hold kept anyone from hearing her.

"Calm down, love. 'Tis only me."

Maggie sagged in relief at the sound of Dracott's soothing voice. She wanted to point out Ravencroft and the lady wearing a cloak, but they had disappeared. Dracott dropped his hand, and Maggie stepped away from her hiding spot. She turned in a circle, searching the darkness for them, but there was no movement anywhere.

"Where did they go?"

"Who?" Dracott asked. "What are you doing alone in the dark woods?"

Maggie walked to the spot where Ravencroft had stood arguing with the lady. Besides the grass flattened from their footprints, there was no other sign of their meeting. Yet she knew they had been there.

"Ravencroft met with a lady in this very spot."

"Are you sure it was a woman?" Dracott questioned.

"Yes. I saw her long hair when the hood fell off her cloak. She also laughed. But I am not sure if you would call it a laugh. It was more of a witch's cackle," Maggie explained.

Dracott's lips twitched. "A witch's cackle. That sounds a bit dramatic."

Maggie stomped her foot. "I am not being dramatic. I know what I saw. Ravencroft stood in this very spot with another lady. It is proof the gentleman cannot be trusted."

Dracott needed to assure Maggie he believed her but still distract her from pursuing this any further. There was only one woman Ravencroft would risk his livelihood to meet in the darkness, where anyone could come upon them. Lady Langdale. She loved to live on the edge and push the boundaries of getting caught. She found pleasure in her status as the most wanted criminal in all of England and laughed over how uncatchable she was. Lady L thought she was invincible.

Her meeting with Ravencroft this evening meant she wanted to proceed with her greatest heist yet, one that would cripple society's security. It would leave them fearing for their fortunes. When the Duke of Colebourne and Lord Worthington exiled her six years ago, she had only grown her force to the likes they held no clue about.

He didn't want Maggie in her cross fire. Lady L would destroy Maggie with her wits alone. He must protect Maggie at all costs. Even if it meant he no longer stood in the shadows hiding his interest. He must state his intentions. It was the only way to keep her safe.

Dracott stepped closer to Maggie and urged her to return to the ball. "I believe you, but this isn't the place for this discussion. Let me return you to your family and tomorrow

I shall call on you. I will seek Lord Worthington's permission for us to take a walk in the park. Are you agreeable to this?"

Maggie peered at him. "Are you serious about your intentions?"

"I am."

Maggie noted the honesty in Dracott's eyes and nodded her acceptance. "I will agree on one condition."

Dracott nodded for Maggie to continue.

"What is your reason for wandering out here?" Maggie asked.

Dracott had a dozen different excuses on the tip of his tongue to answer Maggie. But he had learned early in the years he spent deceiving people that it was best to stick as close to the truth as one could. Then one had fewer lies to keep track of. Not that he wanted to deceive Maggie. His betrayal was for her protection.

"I followed you."

Maggie folded her arms across her chest. "Why?"

Dracott cleared his throat. "In hopes to spend time alone with you."

Maggie's eyes widened. "Oh."

The darkness surrounding them and Maggie's innocent expression led Dracott to step but a breath away from her. All he wanted was to sample a taste of her sweetness. Lady Eden's taunt from earlier played a part in his recklessness. He never could resist a dare in the face of danger. And Margaret Worthington's innocence was the worst danger he could involve himself in.

He tucked a stray curl behind Maggie's ear. "I wonder if you wish for the same. Do you?"

Dracott's intense gaze rattled her senses. It was as if he read her every thought. Which was nonsense. Was it not? She had waited throughout the evening for him to request a dance. But he never had, but she had sensed him watching her from afar. Maggie nodded before she realized she should've kept her interest to herself.

A wicked smile spread across Dracott's lips. "I am pleased you hold the same feelings."

Maggie gulped. "You are?"

Dracott leaned closer and whispered in Maggie's ear, "I am, my dear. More than you can possibly imagine."

"How so?" Maggie whispered.

She had no explanation for how Dracott's closeness heightened her emotions. Maggie held her breath, anticipating his next hushed words. Her body tingled, waiting for him to wrap his arms around her. Her mouth trembled, waiting for the brush of his lips across hers.

"Well, for starters"—he drew her into his arms—"it gives me hope you will enjoy it when I . . . "

Maggie waited for him to finish, but his gaze captured hers, leaving her in no doubt of his intentions. He meant to kiss her. Maggie's eyelids drifted down when his lips softly brushed across hers. A soft sigh escaped, expressing her pleasure. Then his lips swiped across hers again with more pressure.

"Open your lips for me, my little minx," Dracott commanded.

Dracott's tongue stroked across her lips, coaxing them open. Maggie followed his demand, only to have her senses assaulted with the magic of his kiss. He left no doubt with Maggie of his true interest. One kiss turned into another, each more powerful than the last. Maggie's knees weakened from the intensity of his passion.

Dracott caught Maggie against him when she clung to him. He meant to distract her with a kiss, but she overtook his peace of mind with the sweet nectar of her kisses. The little purrs vibrating against her throat inflamed his senses. They made him imagine the delights she would scream when he made love to her. He may have called her a little minx, but he knew she would be a hellcat between the bedsheets.

He kept drinking from her lips. Soon her tongue stroked along his, inviting him to lose himself in her. Everything else faded into the background. Only the two of them existed in this moment.

Soon, a faint call echoed behind him, tearing him out of the spell surrounding them. A warning, stating someone watched him. Not only him, but Maggie, too.

Dracott reluctantly pulled away. Maggie's eyes drifted back open and Dracott wished to capture her gaze and lock it inside his heart forever. It held the look of innocence, wonder, and curiosity all wrapped up in one. A look that would lead to danger by involving her in his life. But it was out of necessity to keep her safe.

Once Maggie regained her balance, he took a step back, placing a respectable distance between them. Not that it mattered, considered they hid in the woods away from prying eyes. Even though the warning sent his way spoke otherwise. Whoever spied on them didn't hold the motive of ruining Maggie's reputation. No. He had his own nefarious motives. Ones Dracott needed to understand and stop before they ruined the lives of the ones he respected. Perhaps even loved.

Maggie held no experience when it came to a man kissing her, but she knew enough that something had distracted Dracott for him to end their kiss. And the distance he placed between them only proved her point. However, when her gaze met his, her eyes captured a different reason. Perhaps she was mistaken about his distraction. Because they reflected a passion he barely kept suppressed. Did their kiss affect him as greatly as it did her?

"Well?" he asked.

"Well what?" Maggie questioned right back.

He stepped into her space once more. "Did you enjoy my kiss?"

The husky baritone of his voice robbed her senses once again. Why did she lose track of herself in his presence? She wanted to answer him with a smirk and perhaps a flirtatious remark, but instead she stood before him like a tongue-tied wallflower. Any other gentleman she would have set him on his heel with a rebuke to keep his distance. However, she only wanted to beg Dracott to kiss her again.

Dracott wanted to draw Maggie on the ground and make love to her. He found her shyness amusing, and it endeared her to him even more.

A second warning lit the air and pushed Dracott to take action. He would have to wait for Maggie's answer. He must get her back into the ballroom.

"Perhaps we should return. I am sure your family is wondering where you have wandered off to," Dracott suggested.

Maggie shook herself out of her fog. She shivered from a chill slinking along her spine. The air changed around them with a sense of danger. Maggie glanced around. Nothing was different, but she felt someone watching them. She looked at Dracott and saw how his demeanor had changed. Yes, they should return with haste. She already needed to make up an excuse for her absence.

"Yes. I agree." Maggie turned and started back to the manor, not waiting for Dracott to accompany her.

Dracott rushed after Maggie to keep her in sight. Her strides took her to the steps leading to the balcony before he reached her. She paused halfway up the stairs and glanced over her shoulder. He didn't understand her stare. It held a mixture of vulnerability and curiosity. However, in the midst, it also held her distrust toward him. It caused him to pause as she continued on.

Waiting for her at the top of the balcony was her sister Eden. He nodded, and Eden returned his nod before guiding her sister back into the ballroom. While Eden thought he fulfilled his duty to Worth, it far surpassed what he and Maggie shared. After this evening, his stance as the assistant who blended into the background following his employer's bidding would end. Tomorrow he must call on Lord Worthington and ask for permission to court Maggie.

But if the lady would agree to the courtship remained to be seen.

Chapter Five

MAGGIE PACED ALONG THE hallway, pausing at Reese's study whenever she passed by. Lord Dracott had arrived over two hours ago and requested an audience. She had grown nervous when Reese and Dracott didn't join them for breakfast. Graham had taken pity on her and offered to find out what they discussed. However, Graham had never returned to inform her of the reason for Dracott's visit. Instead, he remained with them in the study, leading to Maggie pacing back and forth with her impatience. She pressed her ear to the door, hoping to hear what they discussed, but only silence met her.

"Tsk, tsk. Resorting to eavesdropping, are you?" Eden asked.

Maggie glared at her sister's amusement. "How else am I to learn what Lord Dracott wants with Reese?"

"Considering your rendezvous with him last night, it is more than obvious," Eden quipped.

Maggie's eyes widened. "You do not think he is asking for my hand in marriage, do you?"

Eden laughed at her sister's innocence. "No, dear sister. It is my belief that he is asking Reese for permission to court you. While it wasn't wise of Lord Dracott to spend time alone with you last night, he is clever enough not to show his hand with our brothers. The gentleman values his life."

Maggie blushed. "Nothing untoward happened."

Eden narrowed her gaze. "Mmm. I may not have much experience, but I can recognize when a lady has been thoroughly kissed."

Maggie quirked an eyebrow at her sister's slip. "Much?"

The door to the study opened, and the gentlemen stepped into the hallway. Their appearance saved Eden from explaining how much experience she actually had. Maggie took a step forward, only to step back at Reese's frown over her enthusiasm.

Graham clapped Dracott's shoulder. "I told you she was outside, waiting to hear what we discussed."

Maggie shot daggers at Graham for drawing attention toward her. "Nonsense. I only sat with Eden while she waited to talk with Reese."

"Yes. Maggie has kept me company," Eden lied.

Reese glanced back and forth between his sisters. Their telling signs showed how they both fibbed. Maggie twirled her hair around her finger, and Eden bit at her bottom lip. He wanted to shake his head at them, but he didn't want Dracott to know how to detect their flaws. He still hadn't decided his opinion of the gentleman yet to give him any additional weapons to use against his family.

Reese had hesitated when the lord requested an audience and asked to court Maggie. But he noticed how his youngest sister acted differently around Dracott. She kept her wildness contained and appeared concerned with his opinion of her. While he wanted no gentleman to rein in Maggie's uniqueness, it gave him proof that Dracott held a positive influence over his sister.

He also took into account his wife's belief and his brother's opinion of Lord Dracott. Evelyn thought he was a fine gentleman, and Graham held his assistant in high praise. Still, something didn't sit well with him about the lord and he couldn't figure it out. So, against his better judgment, he agreed to the courtship. He would oversee Dracott's visits and how he acted with Maggie at social functions before he gave his seal of approval.

Since his father had passed, it fell on his shoulders to find suitable spouses for his siblings. His father would've only accepted suitors for what he would've gained from their financial wealth. However, he differed. He wanted them to find the love of a soul mate like he had with Evelyn. No other match would do.

"Maggie, Lord Dracott has sought permission to pay court on your behalf. Are you amenable to this?" Reese questioned.

"Reese!" Graham bellowed. "Show a little more finesse."

Eden laughed. "Oh, my. Sorry, Maggie, but I cannot remain. Good luck, Dracott."

After Eden took a few steps away, Reese stopped her. "I thought you wanted a word, dear sister."

Eden looked over her shoulder. "It can wait." She sauntered away before Reese questioned her any further.

Maggie and Dracott stared at each other. They held their own private conversation without speaking a word. His intense regard made it clear to Maggie that he would've pursued her without her brother's permission. After the kiss they shared last night, Dracott would've been relentless in his pursuit, and she would've enjoyed it to the fullest. Dracott gave her a rush she never experienced with just his presence alone. She didn't know if she could survive the full assault, but she wanted to try.

When Maggie gifted him with a secretive smile while her siblings bantered with each other, he knew she approved of his request. Oh, how he wanted to devour her kissable lips. She stood before him with an innocent expression. However, she was a tempting minx. One didn't kiss as Maggie Worthington had to be anything but one. She might be inexperienced, but she held the natural ability to bring a man to his knees with her smile alone. She was like nothing he had ever experienced before. And he had a lot of experience with devious ladies. However, they paled in comparison to Maggie. He held not a clue on how her mind worked, but he was more than willing to learn every facet he could.

"Would you care to accompany me on a walk tomorrow morning before I start my workday?" Dracott asked.

"Yes. I would enjoy that," Maggie answered.

Dracott nodded, then turned to leave. He didn't have a reason to stay. Worthington had already given his permission, and Maggie had answered his invitation. He wanted to spend every available second with her, but he must control his needs. As much as he wanted to learn everything about Maggie, he needed to complete his mission. Because above all, he must protect his identity and that of his brother.

Maggie watched Dracott leave. He cut a fine figure indeed. As Noel would say, most divine. Maggie should've moaned at how she sounded like her nitwit of a sister, but she chuckled instead. This must be what her sister described as smitten. She never believed she would ever feel this way about another soul, which only proved miracles happened, after all.

"Where did Dracott take himself off to?" Graham asked.

Maggie shrugged. He never mentioned it, and she didn't ask.

Reese scoffed. "I gave him permission to court Maggie, and he didn't even ask her for an outing."

"Yes, he did," Maggie defended Dracott.

Reese narrowed his gaze, not approving of a conversation he held no part in. "Did he?"

Maggie nodded. "He asked if I wanted to take a walk with him tomorrow morning before he started his day, and I told him yes."

Reese scowled. "Only with a chaperone."

"Of course, dear brother," Maggie answered before strolling away. She didn't wish to listen to a lecture from her brother on proper etiquette. Her mother's daily nagging already made the fine points of how Maggie should behave and what was acceptable.

"It would appear as if two of our sisters got the best of you today. Which only leaves Noel left to strike with her independence," Graham joked.

"One day a lady will best you and I will sit back and enjoy every second," Reese shot back.

Graham laughed. "That day will never happen."

Reese shook his head. "One day it will, little brother. One day it will."

True to Reese's word, two chaperones trailed a few feet behind Maggie and Lord Dracott on their morning walk through the park. Their chaperones were none other than Reese and Evelyn. Her brother hadn't even given her a chance to argue. Evelyn and Reese had waited with Dracott in the foyer when she hurried downstairs. She wanted to stomp her feet in a tantrum at her brother's interference. But that would never do if she wanted to convince her suitor she was a lady and not a child. Those days were over.

Maggie had spent the early morning hours deciding on an outfit to impress Lord Dracott. When she first arrived in London, she had fought with her mother about the long hours with the dressmaker. Now she needed to apologize to her mother and offer her a token of her appreciation. Because of her mother's demands, she put together an acceptable appearance. She wore a light blue walking dress with a matching pelisse, and adorning her head was a bonnet decorated with yellow flowers. Dracott's eyes had lit with pleasure when they greeted each other this morning, letting her know he approved.

"I apologize for my brother."

Dracott turned his head and smiled. "There is no need. I understand how he only wishes to protect you."

Maggie scoffed. "Protect? No. He is only showcasing his need for control. Also, he thinks I plan to sneak away without a chaperone during our walk since I eagerly agreed to his demands yesterday."

Dracott quirked an eyebrow. "And were you?"

Maggie winked. "Perhaps. But now we will never know."

Dracott laughed. "You are a delight, Maggie Worthington."

Maggie beamed at his compliment. "Thank you, Lord Dracott."

He tilted his head closer but not enough to draw notice. "Crispin," he whispered.

"Crispin," Maggie whispered back.

"I understand 'tis not acceptable for us to speak so informally, but I do hate the proper rules society demands. Perhaps when we are alone, we can speak each other's Christian names."

"Crispin," Maggie repeated, showing him she was agreeable.

"Maggie."

They continued walking in comfortable silence. There was much Dracott wanted to say to Maggie. But the company of others so close by prevented him a chance to do so. It would take some devious moves to allow them time alone, but it was nothing Dracott couldn't manage in the right circumstances.

"Worth invited me to join your family in their box at the theatre tomorrow evening," Dracott informed Maggie.

"Yes, he mentioned his invitation during breakfast this morning. Are you accepting it?"

Dracott smiled. "Yes, I believe I will."

"Excellent."

Dracott glanced over his shoulder to note the distance between them and their chaperones. The Worthingtons had stopped walking and were now engaged, talking to another couple. However, Worthington kept his gaze narrowed on them. With a nod, he made a demand he expected Dracott to follow. Dracott returned the nod, placing his hand on Maggie's arm to halt her walking. When Worthington scowled and took a step forward, Dracott realized his mistake. He never should have touched Maggie. He yanked his hand away, but not before her warmth wrapped around him. Thankfully, Lady Worthington laid her hand on her husband's arm and whispered her own demand.

Maggie stopped when Dracott touched her. Her body trembled with need, hoping for more than a brief touch. However, he denied her when he drew his hand away so swiftly. She raised her gaze to his, struck by the desire simmering between them. When he glanced back at her brother, she understood the reason he pulled away. She didn't need to look behind her to feel her brother's scowl upon them. Reese may be able to intimidate Crispin, but his inferiority had never held much luck with her.

But in his defense, he never had to act in that manner with her. Reese always indulged her as a child with her carefree curiosity. He never placed restrictions on her as her parents did. Now he acted like the overprotected parent, and Maggie only held humor with the situation. To push the limit of her brother's patience, she placed her hand on Crispin's arm and tugged him to follow her to a bench nearby.

Maggie's hand burned through his suit coat. By touching him, she defied her brother and planted him in the path of Worthington's fury. Worth had warned him of Maggie's impish delight in defying Lord Worthington. Now he understood the full implication of the warning. After they sat down, she still refused to remove her hand and slid as close to him as possible. When he tried to slide over, she only moved with him.

"Finally, we have some time alone," Maggie said, sliding her hand down his arm. Her gloved fingers grazed against his.

Dracott glanced again at Worthington to notice the earl grit his teeth in annoyance. "Perhaps we should not anger your brother so early in our courtship."

Maggie laughed. "'Tis only Reese's personality. He likes to intimidate suitors, to make his position clear as our guardian. He acted the same when Ravencroft began his courtship with Noel. Now he never even pays the gentleman a second glance when he comes around. Obviously, my brother is not one to understand the character of a true gentleman such as yourself."

Dracott stiffened at Maggie's opinion of him. She couldn't be further from the truth. He had learned early in life how to change his behavior to mask the situation he found himself in. Yet, with Maggie, he only wished to be his true self and the gentleman she perceived him to be. Also, he didn't want to give Worthington any cause to withdraw his support for their courtship. It was only with the help of Worth's appraisal of his character that Worthington had relented.

He tried once again to separate himself from Maggie, even though he wanted to remain close. This time she didn't follow but frowned her disapproval at him. A small space sat between them now. He turned on the charming smile he used when he wanted to distract a lady from the present. When Maggie blushed a soft shade of pink, he wanted to kick himself for using his technique on someone he cared for. However, it achieved his result of distracting her. He would analyze his emotions later when he had a clear head. Which he didn't think he would ever possess again because Maggie distracted him more than he cared to admit.

"I understand how you wish to defy your brother for your amusement. However, Worthington was none too eager to allow our courtship. It was only with Worth's promise to vouch for my character that your brother allowed for me to call on you."

Maggie nodded, appearing contrite, a trait he didn't care for. He enjoyed the wild, carefree Maggie, not the meek one.

"I wish nothing more than to draw you in my arms and ravish your lips to show you how much of a temptation you are to my state of mind. However, your brother and the other visitors in the park might object."

Maggie's blush turned to a fiery red. "Oh."

Dracott leaned back on the bench, satisfied with her reaction. "Do you understand the position I am in, my wild minx?"

Maggie gulped. "I do now."

Maggie slid across the bench, placing a wider distance between them, so as to leave her brother in no doubt of Dracott's honor. Her act, however, only seemed to amuse her companion. He chuckled at her expense. She fixed her gaze on him and saw that, while he might find amusement with her actions, something darker stirred beneath the surface. From their outing alone, she learned he adapted to any change in their conversation or the surrounding environment. While she saw the desire he held for her, the sense of mystery clinging to him made Maggie only more curious to discover the secrets he held.

Maggie loved mysteries. They were complex and kept her spellbound, not clouding her mind like the romances Noel read. They were as predictable as the titles associated with them. Was the air of mystery surrounding Crispin what drew her to him? Either way, he intrigued her and made her feel special whenever they were together. Her curiosity tugged at her to question why the viscount wanted to pay court to an uncontrollable debutante as her.

Maggie blurted out her thoughts. "Why did you ask to court me?"

Dracott chuckled at her bold question. "I have many reasons."

Maggie's lips puckered as she thought about how to voice her next question. "Do you perhaps enjoy my ability to hold a conversation?"

Dracott inwardly groaned as he stared at her lips. They begged for him to place a kiss upon them. "You are a very intelligent lady."

Maggie shifted on the bench, turning toward him slightly. "Is it because I can dance without stepping on your toes?"

Dracott mimicked her movement on the bench, closing the gap between them. "That is a valid reason. But my reason lies more toward how I enjoy when your hand trembles in mine and how I can, for a brief moment of time, feel your warmth invading my soul when we touch."

When he told Maggie he had many reasons for asking to court her, he had lied. The word many was too tame to describe every reason he wished to spend with her. Even now, she sat before him, too adorable to describe. Yet underneath her adorable persona lay a vixen he wished to draw into his world. A vixen who would keep him sane with her curiosity and give him the security he longed for.

"I shall offer you one more reason about my request before your brother is upon us."

Maggie shifted her gaze to the path to see Reese and Evelyn almost upon them. "And that is?"

"You still have not answered my question and I wish to hear the answer."

"And which question might that be, Crispin?" Maggie's voice dropped to a husky whisper.

The intensity of Crispin's stare did things to Maggie she didn't understand. Her curiosity prompted their conversation, but he dominated it with his bold stare and seductive voice. He turned her into a quivering mess waiting for his next words.

"Did you enjoy my kiss?" He waited right before Worthington and Lady Evelyn stepped in front of the bench before he asked his question, not allowing Maggie any time to answer him.

His question left her flustered because it reminded her of his exquisite kiss, one she had fantasized about countless times, wishing for another one. Now the memory teased her while her brother frowned at her. Maggie didn't need a mirror to see how her face betrayed her thoughts, with a warm blush spreading across her cheeks and along her neck.

Dracott rose when the Worthingtons approached the bench. The earl glared at him, expressing that their walk had come to an end.

Dracott pulled out his timepiece and noted the late hour. As much as he yearned to spend the entire day with Maggie, he must leave. "Thank you for the lovely walk, Lady Margaret. I hope we can enjoy another one soon. In the meantime, I apologize, for I must depart."

"I understand. Thank you, Lord Dracott. I enjoyed our time together. Perhaps I will have an answer to your question when you join our family tomorrow evening at the theater." Maggie offered him an impish smile.

Dracott nodded, a smile tugging on his lips. "I wait with anticipation for your answer." He turned. "Good day, Lord and Lady Worthington."

"Dracott," Worthington grumbled.

"Have a pleasant day, Lord Dracott," Evelyn replied.

A soft sigh whispered past Maggie's lips as she watched Crispin walk away. Crispin. He gave her permission to call him by his Christian name, an intimacy only allowed between married couples. She couldn't wait until tomorrow evening when she would see him again. Hopefully alone.

Worthington scowled. "What was Dracott's question?"

"Mmm," Maggie murmured. Crispin had walked out of her view, but she still kept her gaze on the path he had taken.

"What did Dracott want an answer to?" Worthington demanded, stepping in her eyesight.

Why did it not surprise her that Reese wouldn't allow her one private moment from her courtship? As much as Evelyn tried to soften him, he remained a forcible boulder in her path to freedom.

Maggie twirled the ribbon on her bonnet around her finger. "He only wished to learn my favorite sweet."

Worthington's eyes narrowed when he noticed her act. "Chocolate. 'Tis a simple answer you could have answered in our company. Yet you did not. Which leads me to ask you again. What was his question?"

Evelyn wrapped her hand around Reese's, helping to calm him. "My dear, let us not interfere with Maggie's courtship when they only held a harmless conversation. If it progresses past the point of innocence, then you may interfere however you like. For now, we owe Maggie her privacy. No one interfered during our courtship."

Worthington gazed upon his wife with amusement. "What courtship, my dear?" he teased.

Evelyn blushed. "Exactly."

He lowered his head and kissed his wife. Then he whispered something in Evelyn's ear to turn her cheeks a deep shade of red. "I concede." He focused his attention on Maggie. "For now."

Maggie met her brother's stare, not cowering. She smiled innocently to goad him even more.

Reese shook his head at her. "If you ladies are ready, we can return home."

Evelyn stood on her tiptoes and kissed Reese on the check. "I think Maggie and I will finish our walk. I know you wish to meet with Uncle Theo."

Reese frowned, not wanting to leave. But if he didn't, he would miss the urgent meeting with Evelyn's uncle. "Do not overdo it. Ten more minutes, then make sure Evelyn returns home to rest."

Maggie nodded and watched Reese fuss over Evelyn before striding away. Evelyn sighed the same way Maggie had done when Crispin left. Did Maggie care for Crispin so deeply this early in their courtship? She must because her behavior replicated her sister-in-law's actions too closely.

They walked for a few minutes in silence before Evelyn guided them to sit on the same bench she had shared with Crispin. "Now spill, dear sister."

"My congratulations?"

Evelyn avoided Maggie's gaze. "Whatever for?"

Maggie rolled her eyes. "Please. My brother is doting on you like he did when you carried Mina. So when will I become an aunt again?"

Evelyn's boisterous laughter caused many heads to turn their way. "Oh, you are too clever. However, you hold no proof of your accusation. Your brother dotes on me, regardless of my condition. He loves me."

Maggie sighed. "Of course he loves you. We all do."

"Then, to show your love, you must allow me to be your confidant," Evelyn urged.

Maggie shook her head. "Oh no. Anything I tell you, you will snitch to Reese."

Evelyn sniffed. "I would never betray a sister's confidence."

Maggie cringed. She didn't set out to offend Evelyn. She hated to think she made Evelyn cry because of her own insecurity. "He wanted to know if I enjoyed his kiss," Maggie blurted.

A secretive smile lit Evelyn's face, and her mood changed dramatically. "His kiss? And when, pray tell, did this kiss occur? Because you never left Reese's sight since we set out for today's outing."

Maggie blew out a breath at her gullibility. She'd fallen for Evelyn's trick. "Two nights ago at the Kendrick Ball, I wandered outside and got lost in the woods. Crispin—"

"Crispin?" Evelyn interrupted with a raised eyebrow.

Maggie stayed silent. The more she tried to explain, the deeper she only dug herself in. If she refused to say anything else, then Evelyn wouldn't have any information to share with Reese.

Evelyn regarded Maggie as she remained quiet. It wasn't her place to reprimand her behavior, especially with how she had pursued Reese. However, she could offer her advice and hope Maggie would proceed with caution. While Evelyn thought Lord Dracott an excellent match for Maggie, her husband wasn't convinced yet. He thought the viscount had ulterior motives for his pursuit of Maggie, and she wasn't one to ignore her husband's opinions.

Evelyn drew Maggie's hands between hers. "I will not press you for any more details. Nor will I share what I learned with another soul. However, I warn you to proceed with caution. Only offer Lord Dracott what you do because your heart wishes to, not because of any pressure he applies to act differently."

"Oh, but he did not," Maggie protested.

Evelyn peered into Maggie's eyes and made her judgement that Maggie spoke the truth. "I believe you. May I ask for a promise?"

Maggie nodded.

"Please do not cause a scandal. I fear your brother cannot take on any more added stress." Evelyn winked.

"Whoop!" Maggie shouted with excitement. "I knew it."

Evelyn laughed. "Shh. 'Tis a secret I expect you to keep. We will announce our news after your ball and not until then. We do not wish to take away from your excitement."

"You understand I do not care about that ridiculous ball. Mama is more excited than I am."

"She only wants you to succeed. We all do."

"I promise. No scandal from me this season." Maggie shrugged. "However, I cannot make the same promise for my other siblings."

Maggie stood and helped Evelyn to her feet. They hooked arms and strolled through the park on their return home. When Reese married Evelyn, they had suffered their own tribulations and their marriage survived stronger than ever. They were role models she wanted to replicate with her own marriage, unlike the one of her parents. Oh, her Mama wasn't the one to lay the blame on. That fault lay with her father alone. Reese had walked along the same path until he married Evelyn. The love they held for each other had won in the end.

Maggie wanted someone to love her as deeply and profoundly. Was Lord Dracott the gentleman to capture her heart? Or did he have an ulterior motive he had yet to reveal?

Only a few more kisses would tell.

Chapter Six

D RACOTT ALLOWED NO ONE to intimidate him. However, he desired Maggie like no other woman before, and he couldn't allow Worthington to withdraw his approval. So he parted ways with the Worthingtons and continued to the office. He would bide his time until tomorrow evening. At the theatre, he would find a way for them to be alone together.

Too caught up in his musings, he almost missed seeing Ravencroft stepping into an unmarked carriage in the alley before he reached the office. When the carriage never departed, Dracott snuck closer. Who did his brother meet with? Ravencroft had yet to contact him about a new plan.

Dracott pressed himself against the building, ducking behind some discarded crates. Two men were standing guard on both sides of the carriage. He recognized one of them as Lady L's henchmen. Which meant another guard stood at the front of the carriage, covering both directions. It appeared as if she had gained some new recruits. The one he recognized was a brutal bastard. The brute had beaten Dracott at every opportunity while he grew up.

He gritted his teeth, tightening his fists. Dracott longed to retaliate by knocking the bloke around with a few punches of his own. But he held back, not wanting to give himself away. As far as Lady L knew, he stayed hidden at Ravencroft's estate in southern England. Nor did he want to interfere with whatever dangerous game of deceit Ravencroft played. It would ruin any chance of a future he may hold with the Worthingtons. Lady L would ruin Ravencroft and make an enemy of Reese Worthington with his involvement. Dracott had much to lose, too.

Ravencroft didn't stay inside the carriage for long before disembarking, which only meant he had received his next order.

After the carriage left, Dracott stepped out from behind the crates, blocking Ravencroft's path. "Why in the hell are you meeting with her in broad daylight?"

Ravencroft looked around before answering. "She did not leave me much choice."

Dracott spotted the bruise forming on his brother's cheek. Ravencroft kept looking over his shoulder. Lady L didn't play nicely. That meant her plan wasn't coming together like she wanted. She usually ordered brute force to make everyone follow her orders when she became desperate.

"What does she want you to do?" Dracott asked.

"Nothing," Ravencroft denied.

"The swelling on your cheek speaks otherwise."

Ravencroft brought his hand to his cheek, wincing. "Damn."

A group of gentlemen strolled past them. Dracott pulled Ravencroft behind the crates to hide their meeting.

When no one called attention to them, Dracott tried once again to get answers. "Why have you not made contact?"

Ravencroft leaned his head back against the building. "Because I have yet to formulate a plan that will protect your identity and also destroy that bitch."

"Why did she stick her brutes on you to manhandle today?"

"Because I have ignored her other messages to meet. When you sent me the warning that you witnessed our exchange at the Kendrick Ball, I feared she discovered you were in London. Then, when I saw Lady Margaret with you after I parted from Lady L, I realized how I risked the Worthington ladies with my deceit."

"I kept Maggie away. I do not believe anyone saw her."

Ravencroft scoffed. "You cannot be that naïve. Lady L had eyes watching our exchange. They might not have known it was you, but they knew Lady Margaret stood nearby watching."

"How?" Dracott snarled.

"Because Lady L has made it her mission to know everything there is about Lady Margaret. Even down to her behavior to wander away at balls. She is no longer safe. I fear her life might be at stake for witnessing our meeting."

Dracott advanced on Ravencroft, yanking him by his cravat. "Did she threaten Maggie?"

Ravencroft nodded. He didn't pull away and allowed Dracott his frustration. "If I do not get her the blueprints for the Worthingtons' townhome in a fortnight, then she plans to kidnap Maggie."

Dracott stepped back, running his hand through his hair. "We must confess our involvement to the Worthingtons this instant."

Ravencroft shook his head. "We cannot."

"There must be a way."

"Give me more time. I promise to figure a way out of this mess. In the meantime, Lady Margaret needs protected at all times. Especially at the entertainments the family accepts invitations to. I will try my best to guard her when I can and send word to you of the functions the family plan to attend. You can meet us there. I am owed a few favors that will guarantee your acceptance."

Dracott sighed. "One slight problem with your plan already."

Ravencroft frowned. "What is that?"

"Maggie does not like you."

"Nonsense. She is always polite to me."

Dracott smirked. "Because her mother has taught her to keep her true opinion hidden and to herself. She believes you cover up your true character with lies."

"Damn."

"Do not fret, dear brother. I convinced her to allow me to look into your character to see if I can discover your hidden secrets. Oh, the information I can lay at her feet," Dracott threatened.

"However, you won't because you will not betray your own kin."

Dracott shrugged. "For the love of a good woman, who knows what I might do?"

"You bastard."

Dracott pulled down the sleeves of his suit coat. "Yes. We have already established that fact of my birth. Now I must arrive at work. I am already behind schedule after taking a walk with Maggie and the Worthingtons this morning. You see, I have received Lord Worthington's permission to court Lady Margaret. It appears both of our lives are now financially set for the future."

"You will ruin us with that move."

"'Tis too late. I already set it in motion."

Dracott turned and walked away, leaving his brother to mull over his actions. With his bit of news, Dracott hoped it would prompt his brother to think of a plan for them to survive Lady L's wrath and secure them a future with the Worthington ladies. Because after this morning, he refused to allow Margaret Worthington to be anything other than his wife.

Maggie strolled inside their box at the theater with a calmness far from what she felt. However, she didn't want her family to guess how eagerly she wanted to see Crispin. She kept saying his name over and over in her thoughts. It rolled off her tongue like a verse to a song and wrapped her in an intimacy she wanted to share with him. She had only walked a few steps inside when she noticed him waiting for them to arrive.

He leaned against the railing, holding a flute of champagne. Graham rattled on, probably discussing their latest case. Her brother struggled to break away from obsessing over his work. Their mother worried he would never find a nice girl to marry. If so, his business would be an unwelcome mistress.

However, it would appear Lord Dracott didn't hold the same obsession. His attention had gravitated toward her ever since she entered the theatre box. He lifted his glass in a toast, acknowledging her presence, and his gaze stayed focused on her. Maggie beamed a smile at him, and he returned her smile. Then he walked away from Graham without a word and sauntered over to her.

Maggie laughed at her brother's dumbfounded expression, and Graham scowled at her. However, it didn't take long for someone else to snag Graham's attention. Maggie followed his gaze to see a stunning lady dressed in a revealing midnight-blue gown across the way from them. The lady stood too far away to make out her features, but she had captured Graham's attention. When the lady slipped out of the box, Graham pushed past Dracott on his way out, knocking him into Maggie.

Cool liquid splashed Maggie in the chest and trickled between her breasts. She gasped and tried pulling the fabric away from her body.

"I am terribly sorry, Lady Margaret," Dracott apologized.

He tried not to stare, but the wetness seeped into Maggie's dress and drew his attention to her breasts. The champagne trailed a path down the valley of her chest, and the wetness spread out across her nipples, hardening them into tight buds. He groaned at the sight—and his inconvenient thought of acting on his desire by drawing them between his lips. Dracott pulled out his handkerchief and thrust it into Maggie's hand.

Maggie gasped when Dracott's hand brushed across her nipples. The handkerchief barely covered her chest. She glanced around, mortified, to see if anyone noticed how her body reacted to Dracott's touch. When her family continued to talk amongst one another and paid them no attention, she twisted around so no one would notice.

Dracott tugged off his suit coat and wrapped it around Maggie's shoulders before anyone became aware of her dilemma. However, his gentlemanly attempt brought them more attention than her wet gown ever would.

"Step back from my sister," Worthington ordered. "You have overstepped your bounds with your impropriety."

Maggie turned around, holding the suit coat in front of her chest. "Reese! Apologize immediately. If it were not for Lord Dracott's consideration, the entire theater would witness my disgrace."

Dracott backed away. "My apologies. I did not intend to cause any disrespect."

Worthington snarled. "Your actions speak otherwise."

Maggie stepped between Dracott and Reese. "You misunderstand. Lord Dracott only intended to protect me from any prying eyes."

"It appears he staked his claim on your innocence by marking you as his property," Worthington accused.

Maggie stomped her foot. "Your overprotectiveness is the only act drawing attention to my innocence."

Lady Worthington stepped between her children. "Both of you calm down. You have gained the other patrons' attention with your quarrel. Let me take this coat from you, Maggie, to return to Lord Dracott." She pulled the coat away from her daughter.

"No!" Maggie tried to keep the coat around her shoulders, but her mother's grasp was stronger. She yanked away the coat, drawing everyone's attention to Maggie's dress.

Lady Worthington gasped at her daughter's appearance and swiftly covered her back up again. She fixed her glare on Dracott. "What did you hope to achieve by this act?"

"Mama! As I am trying to explain, Lord Dracott is not to blame," Maggie whined.

Lady Worthington glanced around and saw the patrons in the boxes on both sides of them focusing their attention on the scene. "Explain yourself at once," she whispered.

Maggie nodded. "On Graham's rush to chase after a lady who caught his eye, he shoved Lord Dracott into me. Before Lord Dracott recovered, he accidentally spilled his drink on my dress. Once he saw how the champagne damaged my dress and how it would garner people's interest, he graciously offered me his suit coat. The only one to blame in this incident is Graham. If anything, we owe Lord Dracott an apology for the slander you directed at him that he does not deserve."

Maggie drew in a deep breath from her long tirade and fixed a glare on Reese and her mother. They were too quick to lay the blame on the wrong person, which only led Maggie to wonder if they supported Lord Dracott's courtship. Evelyn and her sisters expressed their delight at the charming gentleman courting her, and Graham never voiced his dislike. However, her mother and older brother's reaction pointed out how they didn't accept his suit. Then why had Reese given his permission for Dracott to court her?

"You have our gratitude for your humble assistance. We shall return your suit coat to you shortly," Lady Worthington apologized.

Before Dracott could accept the apology, Lady Worthington ushered Maggie out of the theater box. Evelyn Worthington stood undecided if she should follow or stay to calm her husband. But her need to see to Maggie's welfare won out. With a whispered warning to her husband, she followed the ladies to the retiring room. Worthington continued with his glare, and Dracott stood tall, not relenting his stance. He kept a neutral expression on his face, not giving away his need to react to the false accusations. He wished to defend himself, but the warning Ravencroft shot at him from behind Worthington kept him silent.

Ravencroft stepped forward and stood next to Worthington. "Very gentlemanly of you, Dracott, to see to Lady Margaret's dilemma."

Dracott nodded and bit his tongue to refrain from calling out Worthington's insensitive reaction to Maggie. While trying to protect her virtue, Worthington only drew speculation about their relationship. Rumors would spread about Maggie's reputation on how free she was with her favors because of this incident. Nothing untoward would be whispered of his name, but Maggie's reputation would become tarnished because she wore proof of her indiscretion, one that had never happened, but the gossipmongers were unaffected by the truth. They loved to tear a lady's name to shame. The longer Worthington stayed silent regarding Dracott in this manner only fueled the rumors to start. If the earl didn't speak soon, it would force Dracott to offer for Maggie this evening.

Worthington must have sensed the urgency to voice his acceptance of the situation. Dracott didn't know if it was because the theatre grew to an eerie silence or if the earl felt a hundred pairs of eyes staring at their box. Either way, it prompted him to step forward and offer his hand.

"Much appreciation for offering your suit coat on my sister's behalf, Lord Dracott. Your kind gesture only proves your honorable character. Our family will forever be grateful for your swift attention." Worthington's voice boomed, causing his words to echo in the vast space.

How Dracott reacted next would set the stage for how the incident would proceed. If he didn't shake Worthington's hand, it would declare he had nefarious attentions and tear Maggie's reputation to shreds, even if that was never the case. However, if he returned the gesture, it gave the earl the power to direct how he wished Dracott and Maggie's courtship to lead, with the earl scrutinizing him more closely than he wanted him to. But it was the only reaction that would guarantee how closely he guarded Maggie. Also, if Worthington withdrew his support, it would put his employment with Worth and Ralston in jeopardy. His entire livelihood depended on him shaking Worthington's hand.

He reached out, and his handshake was firm, relaying to Worthington how he couldn't intimidate him. "No need for your gratitude, my lord. I only stepped in to help, as any gentleman would do for a lady in distress. After all, I am courting the miss, and if I didn't show how much I care for her comfort, how would that appear to Lady Margaret and her family?"

Worthington tightened his grip, snarling behind the smile he portrayed to the watching audience. "A valid point, Lord

Dracott." Worthington surprised him with his next remark. "If all gentlemen acted with such attention to courting, it would ease many parents' and guardians' minds."

"Hear, hear, Worthington," a gentleman declared from the box next to them. "We might have to steal your Lord Dracott for our daughter."

Then all attention suddenly shifted off them and continued on as before. He had never stepped foot in a world like the one before him. Everyone acted as if the situation had never happened, while he was used to staying on guard, waiting for the unexpected to occur.

Before he could react, Maggie strolled back into the box with her mother and Evelyn trailing behind her. She walked up to him and handed him his suit coat. He fought to keep his glance off her chest, but his eyes had a mind of their own.

Maggie smiled shyly. "Thank you, Lord Dracott, for the use of your coat."

Dracott bowed. "I am glad I could help."

Maggie had covered the wet spot with the use of Lady Worthington's shawl. A simple brooch secured the ends high enough so that he wouldn't catch a glimpse of her bosom. He raised his glance to the teasing glint in Maggie's gaze and her slight nod back toward the ladies following her. The minx was a surprise of wonders. She relayed to him how her appearance was the work of her mother. He returned her nod with one of his own and a ghost of a smile. Maggie beamed at their silent conversation. Her smile made it possible for Dracott to relax, putting the incident behind him as easily as the peers surrounding them had.

However, what he didn't realize was how he drew the attention of a certain lady who would deliver the information to her employer. While he hoped to go uncovered for a bit longer, this evening's attention would only draw him deeper into the web of a manipulative lady who would force him to follow her orders.

Lady Worthington urged Maggie past him to sit next to her near the front of the box. Although he had hoped to sit close to her and perhaps hold her hand while no one took notice, that option wasn't a possibility. Instead, everyone took their seats, and Worthington pointed for Dracott to take a seat in the farthest corner. It would appear Worthington meant to banish him as far away from his sister as possible. However, what the earl couldn't prevent him from was admiring Maggie. His viewpoint was direct on the intoxicating miss. One he would enjoy throughout the evening.

Dracott settled into his seat and smiled his enjoyment, which only brought forth another scowl from Worthington. He nodded at the earl, claiming victory for himself once again.

Dracott played a game of risk with the earl. There was much Worthington could rip from him, but to win the love of Maggie, it was worth every risk he attempted. To have her bestow her teasing smile on him every day would be worth it. Not to mention her soft caress and sweet kisses. However, this time, he no longer played a game of entrapping a beautiful miss to become his mark.

This time he meant to claim Maggie as his prize.

Chapter Seven

"YOUR ARROGANCE WILL BE our downfall. Now, because of you, Worthington is questioning if I am suitable for Lady Noel. You must not pursue Lady Margaret after this evening," Ravencroft muttered low enough for only Dracott to hear.

"I will only back away from her if you do the same with Lady Noel."

"Never," Ravencroft hissed.

Dracott bit out a laugh. "Do not tell me you care for the lady?"

Ravencroft never answered him. Dracott shifted his gaze off Maggie to look at his brother. Ravencroft sat with his hands clenched on the arms of his seat, his gaze directed at Lady Noel. Oh bother! The tender expression in his brother's gaze meant only one thing. Ravencroft had fallen for his mark, which only placed the outcome of getting out of Lady L's clutches more difficult to navigate. The bitch would notice Ravencroft's vulnerability and act upon it.

"Why did you have to fall for the lady?" Dracott whispered.

Ravencroft scoffed. "You are a fine one to speak. Lady Margaret has you so enamored you failed to notice that someone has spotted you. Lady L will learn by morning how close you are to her subjects for her revenge."

Dracott tensed, searching the theater for his brother's threat, only to see no reason how he had blown his cover. "Who? Where?"

"She is long gone. Who do you think Worth chased after, causing your slight mishap with Lady Margaret?"

Dracott was clueless as to who Ravencroft talked about. Lady L might think herself invincible, but she wouldn't risk showing her hand this early in the game. The bounty on her head alone spoke of her need to stay hidden. Dracott swung his questioning gaze back to his brother. Ravencroft regarded him with a look of sorrow and sympathy. No. It was impossible. He had secured her release before he and Ravencroft slipped away to his brother's estate. He had made sure of her escape himself.

Dracott shook his head in denial. "No."

"I am afraid so. Your little concubine has found herself once again in our mistress's clutches."

Dracott hissed. "She is not my concubine, nor any other man's. And that bitch is not our mistress."

Ravencroft arched an eyebrow, chuckling. "I always found humor with your denials on the subject of your infatuation. I wonder if Lady Margaret would feel the same once she realizes how she will need to compete with the ghost of your affection."

Dracott gritted his teeth. "Leave Maggie out of this discussion."

"I will for now because she is not the issue at the moment. However, your little display from earlier has drawn unwanted attention our way. Do not think your little protege will not betray you. At this very moment, you can bet she is whispering to Lady L about your arrival in London and the exact description of your appearance."

"Damn," Dracott swore.

He understood Sabrina's desperation if she found herself under Lady L's thumb again. She would betray anyone for her agenda, and he couldn't blame her in the slightest. Everyone, even his own mother, believed his infatuation with Sabrina. However, it was only a cover to keep her protected. The only feelings he held for her were in a brotherly concern. They had placed themselves in many scandalous situations to make his position clear as her protector. She remained an innocent, even if it appeared otherwise. And Ravencroft knew this. He only slandered Sabrina to bait him. Why?

He intended to question Ravencroft, but the play finished its first act and everyone rose, applauding the actors. "We will finish this discussion later."

Ravencroft nodded his acceptance and stepped forward to greet his fiancée. Dracott watched his brother with skepticism. He had observed his brother over the years and had seen how Ravencroft hardened his heart against any emotional attachments. It still shocked him how his brother allowed him to be a part of his life. Now, to see Ravencroft acting besotted with his intended, it left Dracott to wonder if his brother played an act or if he was genuine with his feelings. Only time would tell.

Dracott searched for Maggie but didn't see her. The box had grown crowded with members of Evelyn's family. Soon he found himself pushed near the door. He sighed his frustration. The evening wasn't progressing as he had wanted it to. If he didn't hope to steal a few minutes with Maggie, he would've left. Worthington had made his intention clear by keeping her away from him.

A hand slid against his palm, and warmth invaded his soul at her slight touch. If holding Maggie's hand was their only connection for the evening, it made lingering around worth it.

"There is an empty box with the curtains drawn down the hallway," Maggie whispered.

Dracott needed no other encouragement to sneak away with the enticing minx. He swiped his gaze around the box to see how no one paid them any attention. Maggie tugged on his hand, and he followed her like the besotted pup he was.

The hallway was crowded full of couples visiting with one another, wallflowers hugging the walls like they did at the dances, and a pack of gentlemen debating their skills with dice. They were all oblivious to Maggie leading them away from the Worthington box. When she drew them around the corner and stopped near a closed door, he checked to make sure no one followed them.

Maggie turned the knob, stepped in, and waited for him to follow her inside. He would cross a line if he stepped over the threshold, one he could never cross back over from. However, the vision before him removed all doubts about the course he wished to travel. A path straight to Margaret Worthington's heart.

Maggie waited for Crispin to join her. She risked losing her pristine reputation by tempting him into stealing away with her, and she no longer cared. His honorable intentions from earlier made any doubt she held about his character vanish. Her family might not trust him, but she did. Her mother's endless prattle while repairing her dress had set her on edge. It had been only with Evelyn's admiration over Dracott's actions that her mother had seen reason.

However, her mother had still kept her apart from Crispin during the play. Then Reese had banished Crispin to the back of the box, along with Ravencroft. This had caused Noel to gripe to Maggie throughout the play about how she had ruined her evening. All because Maggie supposedly wanted to draw attention to herself with her selfish need to cause gossip with her actions. Noel blamed Maggie for everything when actually the blame lay with Graham and his need to chase after everything in a skirt. A point she would make clear to her mother during the second act.

For now, she only wished to entice Crispin into a few kisses.

Maggie took a few steps back, luring Crispin to follow her. When he hesitated, glancing over his shoulder, she made a bold move by unclasping her mother's brooch and sliding the shawl off her shoulders to pool around her feet.

"Crispin," Maggie whispered.

Dracott's head whipped around at the sultry whisper that beckoned his attention. He defied his common sense when he closed the door and propped a chair under the knob to keep them from getting caught. And as his steps drew him toward Maggie, his noble intentions from earlier disappeared. However, when his arms wrapped around her and his mouth ravished her lips, Dracott succumbed to the realization of how he was a doomed man destined to fall in love with Margaret Worthington. He would risk any scandal to kiss her sweet lips and worship at her feet. The danger lurking on their horizon was no match for them together.

Maggie was unprepared for Crispin's dominating kisses. She only meant to tease him, but instead she had unleashed what kept him firmly under control. The force of his kiss sent her senses into overdrive. The ache consuming her increased its need to find release. However, Crispin's kisses only teased it further out of her control. When his tongue stroked her lips to open and the brush of his fingers across her nipples set her on fire, her knees buckled from underneath her. Crispen caught her and carried her to a sofa set in the corner.

She clung to him, opening her mouth at his demand. When he settled her on his lap, his kiss slowed. He took his time exploring her with his tongue, gently stroking hers with the softest of touches, only to pull away and trace her lips. Each teasing swipe only built Maggie's need. She whimpered, and he met her reaction with a kiss so profound it left Maggie breathless with its intensity. He molded his mouth against her, drawing on her desire with each stroke of his tongue, leading them into a dance of the forbidden.

Maggie didn't know whether to cry from the depth of the emotions it brought forth or to plead for him to never stop.

Dracott needed to bring himself under control before he unleashed himself upon Maggie's innocence. He didn't know who trembled more from their passion. His hand shook as he caressed her curves nestled against him. But with each touch, her body trembled with her reaction. He drew one kiss after another from her sweet lips.

Hell! There was nothing sweet about her lips. They were a sin he wanted to indulge in for hours on end. No. He needed to indulge in them. He only wished to treasure the unexplainable emotions that were filled with Maggie's kisses.

His hand drifted across her chest. The damp material brought forth the memory of her nipples tightening into taut buds when the champagne spilled across them. He wondered if they tasted as fruity as the wine did on his tongue. His thumb teased a nipple until it hardened under his regard. He lifted his head away from Maggie's lips to watch. With each swipe, her nipples pressed against the fabric. The light material couldn't hide the dark swell of her desire.

Maggie gasped at the intensity spilling from Crispin's gaze on her chest. While she missed his lips upon hers, he captured her attention with his soft caresses. His fingers teased her nipples with each swipe back and forth across them. Maggie moaned from the delicate touch and shifted on his lap, bringing forth a groan from Crispin. He raised his head and their gazes clashed, leaving Maggie in no doubt of his desire for her.

Crispin raised his hand, slid it into her coiffure, and drew her head to his mouth. "You are nothing but trouble. I can no longer resist you."

"Did you even want to?" Maggie's voice trembled.

Crispin paused. She misunderstood him. He never should have spoken his thoughts aloud. "Not since the day I met you."

"Oh." Crispin's answer contradicted his comment, which only confused Maggie. However, he never allowed her to voice her confusion.

His kiss consumed her once again, while his hands slid her gown off her shoulders. The warm air caressed her breasts, but it was Crispin's fingers that lit them on fire. She moaned her pleasure as he trailed kisses along her neck while whispering accolades of devotion about her body. Everything she had read or overheard from listening to Evelyn talk with her sisters never prepared her for the onslaught of Crispin's attention.

His lips trailed to one breast, brushing softly against her nipple, only to retreat to the other breast. Her body trembled in anticipation of the unknown reaction of his desire. He continued the torture by pressing his tongue against the nipple. Then he withdrew the pleasure and repeated the same action on the other nipple. Maggie felt herself slipping out of control but was unable to stop herself from staying sane.

She slid her hands into Crispin's hair and clung to him. "Please," Maggie whimpered.

She didn't know what she begged for, but the sinful stroke of Crispin's tongue held all the answers. His lips on her body was the salvation to her soul.

Crispin heard the desperation in Maggie's tone. It matched the desperation clawing at him to unleash his passion and bring them both pleasure. When her hands clutched at his head, urging him to fulfill their desires, he latched his mouth onto her bud and savored the sweet fruit of the champagne. She tasted heavenly. His need to sample her other delights only increased with each bud he sucked upon. However, he kept himself restrained by focusing on Maggie's pleasure. He was a starving man, and only she could quench his appetite.

Maggie bit her tongue at the sensations coursing through her body. With each pull of Crispin's lips, Maggie floated on a cloud of ecstasy. His hardness pressing into her hip showed that Crispin felt the same. She wished to bring him the same pleasure he brought her, so she shifted back and forth on his lap.

Crispin groaned. "Maggie."

She undid him bit by bit. He was unraveling past the point of no return. But he lost all control to stop himself. His hands cupped her breasts while his mouth continued to dominate her senses. Her moans guided him along. On her sighs, he teased her with a lick. She groaned, and his lips wrapped around a bud and drank its juices. When her hands pulled at his head and held him to her breasts, his lips tightened, sucking harder until she writhed on his lap, easing the ache building in his cock.

A loud gong echoed around him, pulling him from his haze. Silence filled the theater, then the noise of conversations filled the air again. The warning informed them that the intermission would end in ten minutes.

Crispin looked down at the lady spread across his lap. A temptation he swore he would resist while protecting her. However, with one soft whisper of his name from her lips, he had fallen like every man before him. Except Maggie was worth more than everything he risked. As much as he wished to express his thoughts, there wasn't time. He needed to get Maggie back into her family's box before anyone wondered about her absence.

Maggie saw the indecision cross Crispin's features as he drew the dress back over her shoulders. They must return, but before they did, she wanted something from him. "Promise me you will never regret our time here."

Crispin slid his hand over Maggie's cheek. "I will never regret a single moment of our time together. Ever."

Maggie beamed her pleasure at his answer.

Crispin lost himself in her gaze for a brief second before reality set in. With swift work, he set her back to rights. A few tendrils had escaped her coiffure from his ravishment, but they were not enough to draw notice. It appeared only if the pins were loose.

The only task remaining was for them to make their return. With one more brief kiss, he grabbed her hand and hurried to the door. If anyone caught them alone, he would have to suffer through Worthington's and Worth's wrath on ruining Maggie, not to mention Lady Worthington's fury. He shivered from what they would walk into upon their return.

Maggie, while in a blissful daze, wasn't naïve enough not to realize what would happen if anyone caught them. She would either find herself engaged to marry Crispin or shipped back to Worthington Hall in shame. She sensed Crispin feared the same outcome, and she wanted to reassure him. Maggie paused, and Crispin peered in confusion at her.

"I will not allow my brother to force you into a marriage you do not want."

"We may not have a choice."

Maggie narrowed her gaze. "Everyone has a choice to make whatever decision they want. It is up to that person to decide if it is right for them."

Dracott sighed. He wished he held the same optimism as Maggie. But unfortunately, he lived a life where the decisions of others ruled his actions. Even now, he couldn't whisk Maggie away without someone trying to stop him. Dracott prayed she held onto her innocent understanding of life and never experienced the jaded life he led.

He turned toward the door, not agreeing with Maggie, for he couldn't in all honesty. "We must return."

Maggie released a sigh, just as Crispin had done. She expected him to agree with her, but instead he remained quiet. She didn't picture him as a gentleman who allowed other people's opinions to influence the way he lived his life. Perhaps she was mistaken about his character. If she misjudged him on this subject, what else might be false about him?

Before she could question him, a knock sounded on the door. Maggie's eyes widened. Crispin turned and held a finger to his lips to stay silent. He nodded his head for Maggie to step away from the door and hide. She moved against the wall, hidden from any prying eyes.

Dracott opened the door to find Evelyn and Eden standing with impatience. "Ladies."

Eden shook her head at him. "Finally. We have been knocking for an eternity."

Evelyn chuckled. "No, we have not. However, we have no time to waste. Come, Maggie, we must leave. If not, Lord Dracott will find himself a victim of your brother's wrath."

Eden winced. "But his face is too pretty for their fury."

Evelyn nodded. "Exactly. 'Tis why we must hurry."

Dracott didn't quite know how to handle the ladies' amusement. He expected a lecture or at the very least a threat. Instead, they found humor in his predicament. "Let me expl—"

Maggie brushed past him. "There is no need, Crispin."

"Crispin? Oh, I cannot wait to hear more." Evelyn raised her eyebrows at him as she linked her arms through Maggie's and led her away.

Eden smirked. "Neither can I." She turned back toward Dracott. "You need to make your return to the box too, or else Reese will grow more suspicious of your absence. However, wait a few minutes after our return." She strolled away, but not before issuing one more command. Her finger twirled in the air, pointing from the top of his head to the bottom of his feet. "And do not forget to straighten yourself. You look thoroughly ravished."

Dracott closed his eyes in frustration. When he opened them again, Maggie was no longer in his sight. He sensed her disappointment in him and hoped she didn't change her mind about their courtship. Because after holding her in his arms and tasting her charms this evening, it was no longer about protecting her but claiming her as his.

He shut the door before any passerby saw him. Looking down at himself, he noticed his shirt had become untucked and his cravat loosened. He straightened his clothing and smoothed his hair back. He hoped he looked presentable enough to face the Worthington clan. His brother would take one look at him and know what kind of mischief he had gotten himself into. Perhaps if he lingered in the hallway long enough, he could sneak inside the box after the play started again.

However, his luck remained elusive this evening. Once he reached the Worthington box, a hand latched onto his arm and dragged him inside. He tensed, unsure how to act. But when Worth muttered in his ear, "I need your help," Dracott relaxed.

So far, one brother didn't hold a clue about how inappropriate he had acted with his sister. He should feel a sense of guilt, but Dracott meant what he had told Maggie. He didn't regret their time together. And if one suffered guilt, then one must also hold regret.

Worthington stepped in their path, looking at Dracott with suspicion. "Nice of you to join us again, Lord Dracott."

"Sod off, Reese, and stop trying to intimidate my assistant," Worth growled.

Worthington glared at them. "I would not have to if your assistant conducted himself befitting his station."

Worth barked out a laugh. "Station? He is a bloody viscount. A peer. He may be down on his luck regarding having no coin to his name. However, it wasn't long ago that you were in the same predicament. What gives you the right with your pompous attitude?"

Worthington defended himself. "When he acts inappropriate with our sister, it gives me every right."

"From what Eden told me, he only acted as a gentleman with Maggie. An act he corrected because of my fault. Was our sister correct in the information she relayed or did she play me false?" Worth demanded.

Worthington growled. "No, she was correct. However, it does not explain his absence at the same time as our sister's absence from the box during intermission."

Evelyn slid her arm through her husband's. "I already explained away Maggie's absence. She was in the retiring room checking to see if her dress had dried. She wanted to give Mama her shawl back."

"Humph," Worthington muttered, keeping his glare focused on Dracott.

"Dracott has been with me the entire time, so take your inquisition elsewhere," Worth ordered before stomping away to sit down.

The gong sounded for everyone to take their seats and the curtains raised, signaling the beginning of the second act. Dracott nodded at the Worthingtons and joined Worth in the same set of chairs he had sat in during the first act. Ravencroft must have placed himself in the earl's good graces again because he sat next to Lady Noel with a besotted smile on his face. He still didn't understand what to make of his brother's attendance on the young miss.

"I will not cover for you with Reese again. Do not make a habit of sneaking off with my sister. I won't be so forgiving next time," Worth threatened.

"I understand," Dracott bit out.

He didn't mean to take his frustration out on the very gentleman who had saved him from the earl's wrath. However, he didn't take kindly to being talked down to. He understood he had overstepped his bounds, but he didn't need to be reprimanded like a parent would a child.

Worth sighed. "I did not mean to sound so harsh. I only warn you out of rcspect. Reese does not trust easily, and he is protective of our sisters, especially Maggie. As much as she tries his patience, he guards her from the harsh reality of life so that she doesn't have to endure what we did as children. Also, I am aware of my sister's penchant for trouble. She can tempt the very devil."

Dracott cleared his throat and muttered, "That she can."

Worth narrowed his gaze. "Is there anything you wish to share?"

"Not at this time."

Worth nodded in understanding. "For your sake, I hope never."

Dracott never broke his gaze away from the warning. "Point taken."

They sat in silence for a while, neither of them watching the play but weighing what sat heavily in their thoughts. Dracott held no clue what kept Worth preoccupied. It didn't involve Maggie, but what he needed Dracott's help with. Maggie consumed his thoughts, especially with the glances she kept sending his way. However, they no longer held the desire from the kisses they had shared earlier. Instead, her gaze held questions, ones he needed to avoid answering if he hoped to win her hand. He feared if she discovered the truth of his character, she would flee in the opposite direction.

"There is someone I need you to find." Worth's demand broke through Dracott's attention on Maggie.

"Who?" Dracott whispered.

Worth ran his hand through his hair in frustration. "I wish I knew. She always makes an escape before I can gain an introduction."

"Is she connected with our case?"

"No. No. She is an elusive fascination." Worth's voice held a sense of awe that Dracott didn't understand how to interpret.

"I do not understand. Why do you not search for her yourself? That is your profession, is it not?" Dracott quipped.

"I have those other leads concerning Lady L to follow. You are better skilled at locating people who don't wish to be found," Worth explained.

"Like your mystery lady?"

"Exactly."

Dracott sighed. "All right. Give me a description of her and the last place you saw her."

"She was here this evening wearing a midnight-blue gown that clung to her curves, leaving a man's imagination to wonder what lies beneath. Her hair hung past her shoulders in a rich, luxurious mane of glory. Many gentlemen's heads turned when she passed by them, tempting them with her charms. Yet when our gazes connected, they held a look of innocence. Like she played a role of a tempting siren for a purpose. I checked backstage, and none of them were familiar with who I described. I spent the first half of the play searching for her, but she disappeared into thin air, the same way you do sometimes. It was quite uncanny." Worth laughed. "Do you have a sister, perhaps?"

No. He didn't have a sister, but Dracott knew the lady Worth described. He didn't have to discover her identity, but he needed to find where she hid. And when he found her, he would also find Lady L. The source of their investigation. Damn. He had hoped Ravencroft was mistaken on Sabrina's return. Now Worth fancied himself interested in Sabrina. His infatuation would lead toward trouble no one could ever recover from. If Lady L discovered how much Worth found Sabrina desirable, she would use it to her advantage. Sabrina would become a pawn in a game she didn't have the skills to play.

Could this evening get any worse? He decided to leave before it would. He would make Worth believe he would begin his search now. However, he would return home and enjoy a bottle of gin. After the evening he had held, he deserved to turn his mind off and allow the alcohol to numb his senses. Tomorrow was soon enough to straighten out the mess of his life.

"Sorry, I have no sister. If you can make my excuses, I'll see what I can discover while her trail is still fresh."

Worth placed his hand on Dracott's sleeve. "I owe you."

Dracott nodded and shook off Worth's grip. He left the box, not once glancing at Maggie again. Because if he did, he would relent and tell Worth how he didn't owe him. That it was quite the opposite. Dracott owed the Worthingtons an explanation that he fought to keep hidden. With each passing moment spent in Maggie's company and the friendship Worth offered him, it became more difficult not to confess his deceit. However, this evening he kept his secret safe and departed with the knowledge of his true identity and those he cared about.

However, secrets always came to light.

Chapter Eight

DRACOTT WAITED BEHIND THE tree until Worthington's carriage traveled out of sight. Then he stepped onto the walkway and climbed the steps leading to the townhome. He would admit he was a coward by avoiding Worthington, but the pounding in his head thanked him for avoiding the earl.

His late-night indulgence had left him sleeping past noon and waking in a miserable fit. However, he rose and started his day with a purpose. A purpose that was so far full of lies. He had a messenger deliver a missive to Worth, explaining his absence with false information about his search for Worth's mystery lady. Then he waited for Worthington to leave for his afternoon appointments. Dracott had learned the earl's schedule from his days of shadowing the earl and his family when he arrived in London, searching for Ravencroft. There wasn't much he hadn't learned about the family.

He knocked on the door and waited for Worthington's butler, Rogers, to appear. The man didn't make him wait long. However, he refused to announce his visit.

"Lord Worthington has given me instructions for when you called. I am to ask for you to return when he is at home," Rogers stated.

Dracott nodded, expecting this reaction when he visited. "I understand. If you would be so kind to give this to Lady Worthington and Lady Margaret, I would appreciate it."

Rogers reluctantly took the box from Dracott. "I see no harm in your request. Good day, Lord Dracott."

Dracott smiled. "Thank you, kind sir. I hope your day brings goodness to you, too."

Dracott took his leave with grace and couldn't help but smile. The earl must feel threatened about his intentions since he had placed an obstacle in his way to see Maggie. However, it was one that he would maneuver around in time.

He had walked a few blocks before he sensed someone following him. Dracott stopped to allow a governess to pass him with her young charges and looked behind him. He noted nothing out of the ordinary to draw upon his curiosity, so he continued on.

When he strolled into the busier part of the city, instinct kicked in for him to flush out his follower. He slipped inside a bookstore and headed to the back of the shop. The twinkling of the bell alerted Dracott of another visitor. After the culprit drew closer, he slipped through the back door into the alleyway. Once there, he hid in between the empty crates and waited for his prey to present themselves.

He didn't have to wait long when the street urchin passed by him, not noticing his hiding spot. The lad glanced around, searching for him. When he didn't see him, he let out a whistle and continued on. Dracott knew the whistle well because he had taught it to the lad. He stayed hidden, waiting for the goons to come out of their hiding places.

Before the lad reached the end of the alley, the two henchmen grabbed the boy and threatened him with their insults. Then they threw him on the ground and stalked toward the carriage that was waiting a few feet away.

After opening the door, one henchman turned to taunt the lad. "The madame expects the information by nightfall. If not, then I get to choose the torture for your punishment." The henchman laughed.

Most would have cringed at the brute's glee. However, the lad lifted his chin with defiance. Dracott shook his head at the youth's determination. That determination had always landed them in trouble. The scene before him indicated that Lady L had discovered Dracott was in London and planned to exploit his attachment with the Worthingtons to her agenda. Ravencroft had warned him of this, and he had ignored him in his revenge to bring the lady to justice. There was more at stake than simply protecting Maggie. His friend, who didn't cower to the henchman, needed his help too. Would this nightmare ever end?

After the henchmen climbed aboard the carriage and it took off, the lad scrambled to his feet, dusting off his trousers. He ambled his way back down the alley toward Dracott, stopping near the crates. He sat down and leaned against one, taking an apple from his pocket. To any passerby, he looked to be a young lad eating his lunch.

He crunched through the apple. "The coast is clear."

Dracott sighed. "You know it is not."

"I only had two of them following me. They left with her."

"Ren, I have explained this to you before. Another one stays far enough away so you do not see them trail you."

"Either way, I must give her information on your whereabouts and confirm it is you who courts Margaret Worthington." Ren bit out a laugh. "Courting the mark? Brilliant of you, Dracott. Has the lady fallen for your charms yet?"

"Lady Margaret is not up for discussion," Dracott growled.

"Oh là là. It appears you are as smitten with the miss as Ravencroft is with the sister," Ren drawled.

Dracott slid down against the brick wall. "It is not what it appears." He hoped his denial would convince her.

"What? Are you trying to tell me she is different from the other ladies you conned? That she actually means something to you?" Ren scoffed. "Please, Dracott. I have seen you in action before, and you play her like every other lady who had the misfortunate luck to entangle themselves in your charms."

Dracott remained silent. No matter how much of a bond he shared with Ren, it didn't mean he trusted his friend. Ren would betray him to keep from becoming a victim of Lady L's vindictiveness.

Ren took another bite. "Your silence speaks for itself."

"Why did you not stay hidden?" Dracott hissed. "Do you not care what I risked for your safety?"

"You risked nothing but a cosy bed at your brother's estate, securing your own freedom." Ren scoffed. "While you left me vulnerable, waiting in the open for Lady L to find me."

"I secured you a new identity in a village where Lady L would never find you. You were to wait for my return," Dracott argued.

"A lot good that did. You placed me in the same village with another enemy. An enemy who was tired of running from Lady L. So I became a sacrifice. A trade to secure one enemy's immunity for another."

Anguish settled over Dracott at the position he had placed his friend in. Ren didn't need to mention who the enemy was for him to know the villain's identity. "My mother has made her return," Dracott guessed.

"Yes."

His mother hated the bond Dracott shared with Ren. She used her manipulations to keep them apart, only to fail at every opportunity. And he had delivered Ren to his mother's doorstep with his abandonment. Now Ren must confirm his identity to survive. He felt the rush of wind attempting to knock him off the ledge increasing.

"Ren?"

He waited for a reply, but none was forthcoming. While he tried to come to terms with his betrayal, his friend had left. Now he must figure out how not to become trapped with Lady L's latest heist. Ren would confirm his identity to avoid the henchman's torture. Before long, the witch would summon him to her lair.

He held too many cards in his hand this time around. His conscience battled with him to come clean, but his instincts told him to play his cards close to his chest and only trust those who wouldn't betray him. It wasn't as if he didn't trust Worth and Ralston, but he didn't want to jeopardize their safety and those of their families. They were already at risk, as it was.

Dracott was pulled in too many directions to count. He worried Maggie doubted him and he wanted to reassure her. Worth wanted him to trail a lady Dracott could never reveal the truth about. Worth and Ralston both expected him to help bring Lady L to justice. Lord Worthington suspected he held ulterior motives toward Maggie and watched his every move. Maggie's mother disapproved of his behavior from the evening before and now treated him with hostility.

Also, he must learn of the secrets Ravencroft kept from him. And now with Ren's return, he would worry over the abuse his friend would suffer from because of Dracott's foolish attempts at securing their freedom.

Which left him to deal with the matter of his mother. He should've known she was involved again. How else could Lady L return to town undetected?

What course of action should he take?

Maggie kept watching the door for Rogers to announce any visitors. But the door stayed closed. Mama and Evelyn had sat for the past hour with their heads bent together, whispering between themselves. From their covert glances, she knew they discussed Dracott. She hadn't thanked Evelyn for covering for her, but she thought Evelyn supported Lord Dracott's courtship, even though Reese was reconsidering and Mama agreed with him. However, Evelyn continued to make fine points toward Dracott's character and Mama appeared to relent.

But did Maggie want her to? She had doubted Dracott herself when he never responded to her comment. Then he had abruptly left during the second act without paying his respects, an action that had infuriated Reese and injured her pride. Of course, Graham had made excuses for the hasty retreat, which left Maggie to wonder if Graham had threatened Dracott.

Maggie sat forward in her chair with indecision. Did she pass judgement too swiftly when his actions might've been out of his control? She knew how overprotective her family was with her. While she sat with a bruised ego, Crispin could be out of employment. Which left her to wonder why he worked for Graham. He was a viscount who dressed in fine clothing, not in the state of a penniless peer.

Maggie ran her hands through her hair in frustration. She held so many questions but didn't know who she could trust to give her the correct answers. Every time she made an excuse for him, another question arose. She was more confused than ever. She needed to find Crispin. Perhaps if she confronted him with her doubts, he would help ease her conflicted thoughts.

But how was she supposed to find herself alone with him? Her mother watched her like a hawk. If not her mother, then Reese occupied her time by tempting her with visits to Tattersalls or rides through Hyde Park. They already taken a ride early this morning, and before he left for his appointments, Reese had promised Maggie another ride upon his return.

"Your eagerness will only increase Mama's negative opinion of the poor bloke," Eden murmured, sitting in the chair next to Maggie.

Maggie whipped her head to the side. She didn't realize her sister had sat down next to her. She straightened in the chair and flipped the page in her book. "I have no clue what you are implying."

Eden chuckled low enough so as not to draw their mother's attention. "You are fidgeting more than usual."

Maggie continued with her denial. "I only wish to sit upon a horse, not stuck in this dress, waiting for Mama's next direction. 'Tis all."

"Balderdash. Confess, little sister. What has you tied in knots? Is it Lord Dracott?"

Maggie sighed. Since Eden had helped Evelyn cover for her disappearance last night, then perhaps her sister could help her see reason. "Why has he not shown? Did he leave early last night because Graham threatened him? Is he sincere in his attention or am I only a distraction? Why is Mama changing her mind about Crispin's character?"

Eden smirked her enjoyment at Maggie's frazzled reaction. "Perhaps because our brother has left explicit instructions with Rogers not to allow him entry."

Maggie narrowed her gaze. "He wouldn't."

Eden nodded that he indeed would.

"That explains the sudden invitation to take me to Tattersalls. He has avoided letting me accompany him all season because of Mama's insistence on how a proper lady shouldn't be seen examining horseflesh. Now he offers to take me on the morrow."

"I overheard him talking to Mama. He hopes he can offer you enough distractions to entertain you so that you will forget your infatuation with Dracott."

Maggie's look held exasperation at her family's attitude toward her feelings for Dracott. "'Tis not an infatuation."

Eden quirked an eyebrow. "What is it then? Do you love him?"

"How can I love someone when I've not been given the chance to become better acquainted with him?"

"Excellent point." Eden glanced over at their mother. "Regarding your other questions, I can only answer with what I speculate. First, Graham did not threaten Dracott. He ordered him to follow a lead, and Dracott needed to follow Graham's command. I am not sure of Dracott's financial situation, but I am under the impression he needs to support himself with employment."

"That explains Graham, but what about Mama?"

"Ah, Maggie. You are her baby, and she doesn't want to let you go. No gentleman will ever be good enough for you."

Maggie harrumphed. "Then why insist on my involvement in this year's season?"

Eden laughed. "Because Mama enjoys attending all the entertainments. Papa never allowed Mama to experience the seasons when he lived. He forbade her to visit London and forced her to remain at Worthington Hall. She missed her friends and the enjoyment she finds from the balls and musicals. You cannot fault her for wanting to attend the different festivities."

"But she could've delighted in those activities without me."

"We receive more invitations to certain balls because Mama is debuting a debutante such as yourself," Eden explained.

Maggie sighed with disappointment in herself. While she grew irritated with her mother over Dracott's treatment, she had misunderstood what a season meant to Mama. She had sacrificed her life, protecting her children from a temperamental husband, only to suffer disgrace from his passing. The least Maggie could do was take part in the season. While she still wished for Dracott to court her, she made a promise to herself to accept more dances from the other gentlemen who attempted to meet her.

"As for Lord Dracott, he is as smitten with you as you are with him. His gaze when he stares at you holds the same passion as Reese does for Evelyn. You must understand the position he is in and how he must watch his every step."

Maggie pouted. "This business of courtship seems so senseless."

"That it does, dear sister. One I am glad I do not have to endure," Eden boasted.

"Oh, but Mama will make you eventually," Maggie warned.

"Mmm, we shall see."

"We shall see what?" Noel asked, drawing the other ladies' attention onto them.

Maggie swung a guilty expression at Eden. With a slight shake of her head, Eden warned Maggie to stay silent and that she would handle Noel's interruption. "We shall see if Lord Finkelstein asks for my hand in a dance tomorrow evening at the Harrisson Ball."

Noel's eyes lit up at Eden's discomfort. The earl had been a thorn in Eden's side for the season. At every opportunity, he attempted to woo her, even trying to catch her unaware to compromise her. He fancied her and thought she would make an excellent mother to his four children. Every time he drew near to their circle, shudders would rack Eden's petite frame. At least Reese and Mama found him in poor taste and refused him any association with Eden. Still, he was a bother she had to deal with on certain occasions.

Mama tsked. "Unfortunately, he will. The gentlemen are acting out of character this season. They do not realize how they step out of bounds with their behavior."

"Mama!" Maggie objected.

Mama sent Maggie a warning glare not to give her opinion on the matter. It would appear Evelyn's reassurance concerning Lord Dracott had done no good. Maggie swung her questioning gaze at Evelyn, who shrugged and offered an encouraging smile.

Before Maggie voiced her opinion, Rogers entered, carrying a box in his hand. He walked over to Mama and handed it over. "For you, my lady. The gentleman wanted me to deliver this to you, along with his letter."

Maggie leaned forward and saw the box of chocolate from Sampsons. "Do you have an admirer, Mama?"

Mama blushed. "Nonsense."

Mama opened the missive and read the note. It was an apology from Lord Dracott, one she hadn't been expecting since his impolite departure the evening before. However, he went into great depth to explain his departure and his intention to protect Maggie. His apology matched what Evelyn had tried to convince her of a few moments ago. She sighed. As much as she wanted Maggie to experience the season, she also noticed the attraction simmering between her daughter and Lord Dracott. Was it wrong of her to worry so much?

She set the note down and opened the box to see it full of her favorite chocolates. Not only her favorites, but Maggie's too. The gift was an expression to make his apologies to each lady. She had noticed the longing in her daughter's eyes all day, as well as the doubt. It was time she put her differences to the side and accepted Lord Dracott as Maggie's choice. Her reasons for denying them a chance were her own selfish ones.

Maggie was her youngest child, and she wished to protect her from the evilness in the world. She was a kindhearted soul whose love of animals kept her innocent from the harsh realities of life. She didn't remember the rants her father delivered, like her older children. But shielding her from life experiences wasn't healthy for the girl, either.

She drew out a chocolate and took a bite. After moaning at the delicious sensation of the creamy center melting in her mouth, she passed the box and letter over to Maggie. Her daughter looked at her in confusion, and she nodded for Maggie to read the letter. After Maggie finished reading, her expression filled with hope. Lady Worthington smiled her acceptance, and a smile lit Maggie's face as she had never seen before, reassuring her that she had made the right decision.

"Please show Lord Dracott in," Mama directed Rogers.

Rogers appeared unsure of himself. His direct orders from Lord Worthington to refuse the gentleman were clear. However, everyone knew Lady Worthington overruled her son in the matters of Lady Margaret. "I am afraid I have sent him on."

Lady Worthington arched her brow. "Why would you do that?"

He gulped. "Lord Worthington left instructions that Lord Dracott was not welcome unless he was present."

Evelyn shook her head at Reese's interference. "I hope Lord Dracott did not make a fuss at your refusal." She sent a wink in Maggie's direction.

Maggie frowned, not understanding what Evelyn was playing at.

"No, my lady. He stated how he respected the order and would abide by Lord Worthington's instructions. He only asked that I deliver his offerings," Rogers explained.

"Why did you not refuse them?" Evelyn asked.

"Because Lord Worthington never mentioned how I should proceed if Lord Dracott delivered anything. He only ordered what I was to say to the gentleman when he arrived."

Mama chuckled at the servant's defiance. "How very clever of you, Rogers."

Rogers bowed. "Thank you, my lady."

Rogers winked at Maggie when he walked out of the parlor. She smiled her gratitude. It pleased her how many people worked to help her achieve her happiness.

"Well, it would appear Graham is keeping Lord Dracott occupied with a task. However, a gentleman needs to eat, does he not?" Mama asked Maggie, and Maggie nodded. "Excellent. I shall send word to Graham to bring Lord Dracott to dinner since we are dining in this evening. It will give you a chance to spend time with Lord Dracott and for us to extend our gratitude for his gallant act last night. Also, we owe him an apology for our harsh treatment."

Maggie rushed over to her mother and knelt at her feet. "Thank you, Mama."

Lady Worthington brushed a hand over her daughter's hair and smiled fondly at her. "I only wish the very best for you, my dear."

Maggie stayed curled at her mother's feet, while the ladies enjoyed the box of chocolates Lord Dracott had sent them.

They teased Eden of Lord Finkelstein's infatuation, and Mama shared stories of her own season. Evelyn and Noel commented on what Maggie should wear for dinner. The entire time, Mama enjoyed the warm atmosphere. Evelyn had been a wonderful addition to their family, and Ravencroft seemed to fit Noel's flightiness. It was only fair for her to open her arms to Dracott. She didn't know his story but wished to learn about him to make her daughter happy.

After all, she only wanted happiness for all of her children.

Chapter Nine

D RACOTT WAS UNPREPARED FOR what to expect when he
arrived at the Worthington townhome for dinner. The
invitation Graham had thrust into his hand before he left the
office still surprised him. He had expected to continue making
amends before the Worthingtons accepted him into their fold
again. However, he now sat at their dining room table, sharing
an intimate dinner with Maggie's family.

Lady Worthington had astonished him when she greeted
him warmly by thanking him for his gift of chocolates. She
continued with her surprises by inquiring if she had his
permission to call him by his Christian name. She told him
how she detested the formality required amongst peers and
preferred everyone to call each other by their first names
when it was only their family present. Lady Worthington even
granted him permission to call her Meredith.

Maggie was as surprised herself and offered him a smile
filled with shyness whenever their glances met, which was
often because she sat across from him. Disappointment had
settled over him when he first sat down between Evelyn and
Eden. However, Maggie was a magnificent sight to watch. She
teased her family members with as much enthusiasm as they

teased her. Her titillating laughter soothed his soul from the trying day he had suffered through.

Even Worthington relented his stance by shaking his hand when he arrived. It appeared the earl respected him on how he had handled himself earlier when Rogers denied him entrance.

Dracott sat through most of the meal in silence. The Worthington family astounded him with their teasing nature and acceptance of each other. He had witnessed many meals with them in this regard. However, the more time he spent with Maggie, the more he realized it wasn't a facade. They truly enjoyed each other's company. Even Ravencroft sat relaxed and joined in with the conversation flowing around the table.

He had never experienced a family setting such as this. Dracott held no memories of his father, and his mother held no maternal feelings at all. The only attachment he had with family was the mangled affair he held with Ravencroft, a brother who held no clue on how to deal with him. Ravencroft had every right to turn his back on him. Dracott was a bastard born to the mother who had abandoned Ravencroft's father. Yet Ravencroft protected Dracott from the harsh realities of life to the best of his abilities.

Laughter floated around him as Worth teased his sisters. Dracott smiled when they flipped the teasing back at Worth. Instead of retaliating, Worth laughed in amusement along with them.

"Please forgive my children, Crispin. They have no bounds when they rile each other," Meredith stated.

Crispin smiled. "I quite enjoy the entertainment."

"Do you share the same amusement with your own siblings?" Evelyn asked.

Crispin's smile turned wistful. "Unfortunately, no. I am an only child."

All the ladies reacted with the same expression of sorrow. "Ahh."

Ravencroft coughed into his napkin, drawing the attention toward him. "My apologies. My meal went down the wrong pipe."

Dracott bit back a sigh. He knew it bothered Ravencroft when Dracott never acknowledged him as his brother. With the danger surrounding them, he couldn't risk revealing their relationship. He had arrived in London with a false identity and told Worth that he had no living kin. His lie had convinced Worth to employ him to help capture Lady L. He had assured Worth that there would be no repercussions of retaliation on his family's part if he were to die. He must continue with the deceit.

"Shall we adorn to the drawing room for dessert?" Meredith inquired.

Evelyn clapped. "A wonderful idea. I will gather Mina for our evening's entertainment."

"Excellent," Meredith exclaimed, leading everyone away from the table.

Reese followed his wife up the stairs to gather their daughter, while Noel hooked her arm through Ravencroft's, leading him along. Graham linked his arms with his mother and Eden, which left Crispin to escort Maggie. He held out his arm, and she accepted it with another shy smile.

"I am delighted you accepted Mama's invitation," Maggie whispered.

Crispin squeezed Maggie's hand. "I would not have missed a chance to see you, regardless of your family's company."

"I feared they scared you away with their actions."

Crispin kept with his assurances. "It will take more than a brother's protectiveness and a mother's need to cling to her youngest child to keep me away from you."

Maggie leaned her head against his arm. "I am glad you understand them. While I wish nothing more than to defy them and spend time alone with you, I find comfort that you don't make me choose."

"I would never force you into that predicament."

The way Maggie laid her head against him showed Dracott how much she trusted him, and it warmed his heart. Even if it was under false pretenses on his end. However, he couldn't change his course. He would treasure this feeling before someone ripped her from his grasp. He hated to betray Maggie's trust, but he only did so to keep her safe. It was what he told himself to justify his deceit. Hell! If they had the chance, any gentleman would act the same.

She moved her head off him before they entered the drawing room. "I know."

Maggie dropped Crispin's arm before her mother noticed. Crispin stood in her family's good graces, and she didn't want to give them any reason to withdraw their friendliness. Eden's comments from this afternoon resonated with Maggie. Crispin didn't hold the luxury to disregard an order from an employer when he depended on the livelihood. Maggie decided to trust Crispin because he hadn't given her any reason not to.

She settled on the sofa and patted the spot next to her inconspicuously. Crispin sat down, keeping a respectable distance between them. He settled back against the cushions with confidence but not too arrogantly on pulling one over on her family. No. It appeared as if her family's acceptance relaxed him.

When Mina ran into the drawing room and jumped on Worth's lap, Crispin laughed at the toddler's exuberance. The room joined in with his laughter. Once Mina realized she held the room's attention with her display, she tried to gain the same reaction with Ravencroft. When she did, she moved on to Crispin next. Only this time, she settled on his lap, content, sucking on her thumb.

When the servant served dessert, Evelyn attempted to persuade Mina to sit on her lap. However, Mina whimpered her denial and laid her head on Crispin's shoulder.

"Come, Mina. Let Crispin eat his cake," Evelyn urged. Mina shook her head.

"She is fine. Let her rest a spell. She should fall asleep soon. Enjoy your cake. I will eat mine soon enough," Crispin assured Evelyn.

If his offering of chocolate didn't warm her mother's heart toward him, then his unselfish act alone did. Maggie saw her mother's gaze soften toward Crispin. He had won her mother over. Maggie swung her attention to Reese. He was the only family member left who held out an objection. However, his guard appeared to slip with his daughter's warm acceptance of Crispin. Who knew a child held the ability to influence her father to set his prejudices to the side? Reese shifted his gaze and focused on Maggie, giving her a slight nod to show his acceptance. Maggie beamed her approval at him, and he smiled at her with a father's pride.

Worth stretched his legs out in front of him, balancing his plate across his stomach. "Since Dracott skillfully charmed his way into you ladies' hearts, then he can stand in my place for all the upcoming entertainments."

"You will not abandon your obligations by unloading them on your sister's suitor. He may be your employee, but when he accompanies us, it will be as Maggie's companion, not as your replacement," Reese ordered.

"Ahh, dictatorial as ever," Graham muttered.

Reese smirked. "How else will we get you settled?"

Graham shrugged. "Perhaps because I see no need to settle my affairs with a bride."

"I wish for all my children to find their soul mates," Mama argued.

"I shall pass with that endeavor," Graham continued.

"Why do you remain stubborn on this topic?" Mama asked.

"Because he already has his eye on someone, Mama," Maggie teased.

Mama gasped. "Oh! Who is she?"

Maggie shrugged. "I do not know who she is. He chased after her at the theater. 'Tis why Crispin came to my rescue. She caught Graham's eye, and he raced off to capture her attention. But one has to wonder if she eluded him. I would have to say yes since he returned to the box wearing a dejected expression."

"Clam it shut, Mags," Graham warned.

Maggie giggled. "Ahh, 'tis no fun when you are the one to be teased, is it, dear brother?"

Graham shook his head at her. "You will pay, squirt."

Maggie's eyes twinkled. "I cannot wait."

She relaxed back into the cushions, pleased with how the evening was playing itself out. Even watching her sister fawn over Ravencroft didn't annoy Maggie. She still didn't trust the gentleman, but he no longer troubled her thoughts. Perhaps the attention her sister received from Ravencroft made Maggie jealous. Ever since Crispin called on Maggie, she had lost interest in her soon-to-be brother-in-law.

Maggie tilted her head to the side and found Crispin staring at her niece, who was asleep in his arms. She didn't understand the depth of his gaze. There were no words for the emotions pouring forth. It held wonderment, joy, contentment, all wrapped up in a sense of sadness. While she observed him, the depth of her own emotions swelled in her heart. She realized she had fallen in love with him. Would he gaze upon his own child in the same regard? If so, would she hold the honor of being the child's mother?

Maggie received the answer to her question when Crispin's head rose, and their gazes connected. Yes. His stare portrayed what she herself felt. They needed no words shared between them to communicate the depth of their feelings for one another. She wished they were alone so she could kiss him. She wanted to be one with him. To lie in his arms while he worshipped her and she would worship him in return.

Crispin watched the emotions flit through Maggie's stare. Its intensity held a profound effect on his soul. Her eyes expressed her every thought. He wished they were alone so he could show her how much he reciprocated what she felt. He would leave no part of her unkissed. As he worshipped at her feet, he would caress every delectable inch of her. But most of all, he wanted to hold her in his arms and declare his love for her. He had fallen and fallen hard.

He dragged his gaze away from her for fear of ruining her family's forgiveness. If any of them noticed the passion simmering between them, they would kick him out and forbid him any contact with her. Instead, he focused on the little girl in his arms, an innocent he would do everything in his power to protect. Even sacrifice himself, if need be. He raised his head again and encountered Ravencroft's stare. His brother must hold the same opinion because he glanced at the child before meeting his stare again. His look held the same determination. At least they agreed upon this matter.

He gave Ravencroft a slight nod, indicating his need to talk with him. His brother signaled with his own response.

"It would appear I was correct. She has fallen asleep," Crispin whispered.

"Oh dear, she has the sweet mite," Meredith murmured.

Reese walked over to him and gathered his daughter in his arms. "We shall say our goodnights. Thank you, Ravencroft and Dracott, for joining our family for dinner. We hope to share many more with you in the future."

Reese's comment spurred the rest of the family to murmur their agreement. His statement declared his approval for the two gentlemen to join their family. Two gentlemen who stood on the verge of destroying their trust with lies. They needed to confess their deceit, but they kept sinking in deeper the more they tried to dig out.

After Reese and Evelyn retired for the evening with their daughter, Ravencroft rose. "With your permission, Meredith, may Dracott and I escort Noel and Maggie for a stroll around the garden?"

Meredith bestowed a smile on Ravencroft. "That sounds like a lovely idea. Enjoy yourselves."

Dracott stood and held out his hand to help Maggie rise. Once again, a shy smile graced her lips. They followed Ravencroft and Noel out into the warm night. The weather had grown warmer as the evening passed.

"Mina looked like an angel in your arms. You have a way with children," Maggie said.

"She is a sweet child," Crispin replied.

"Do you want children of your own?" Maggie asked.

He had never pondered the thought before. If someone had ever asked him, he would've answered with a resounding denial. He refused to bring a child into the threat of uncertainty always hanging over him. However, the thought of Maggie being pregnant with their child stirred something in Crispin. The image of her holding their child only made the emotion more intense, and his answer was simple to make.

"Yes." He stopped walking and turned to her. "Do you?"

Maggie nodded, too choked up to give him an answer.

He returned her nod, understanding the emotion their questions sparked.

They resumed their walk again and stopped near the fountain. Ravencroft and Noel had settled on the bench with their heads bent close together. He tried not to stare, but his brother's behavior astounded him.

"It is sickening to watch." Maggie groaned. "Their behavior is so sappy."

"Is it now?" He tugged Maggie behind the fountain for some privacy.

Before Maggie could answer, Crispin pulled her into his embrace and swallowed her comment with his kiss.

When he let her up for air, her adorable, amused expression caused him to question, "Too sappy?" before pressing his lips against hers again. Only this time, he drew out the kiss with agonizing slowness.

He lifted his head and swiped his thumb across her lips. "Personally, I enjoy sappy. But if you do not?"

Maggie darted her tongue out, surprising Crispin. He wasn't the only one capable of teasing. "If only your kiss was sappy enough."

Crispin's eyes darkened. Her sass only increased his desire to make love to her. Her tongue continued to trace over his thumb, drawing it deeper into her mouth. She enticed him into her web.

"I cannot allow any rumors to spread that I cannot fulfill your requirements for sappiness."

His thumb pulled her lip down as he lowered his head. His tongue struck out inside her mouth, showing Maggie the many depths he wished to possess her and draw her into his soul. He left her with no doubt of his intention going forth. She whimpered into their kiss and then met him stroke for stroke. His hand cupped her cheek, drawing her lips under his while he ravished her with one kiss after another.

He forgot his whereabouts when someone behind them cleared their throat. Not once, but again with increasing annoyance. He wanted to swat at the disturbance, but the forceful grip on his shoulder brought him to his senses. With reluctance, he pulled his lips away from Maggie's and dropped his hands. Someone had caught them. He only hoped whoever gripped his shoulder wasn't the one who would take away what he most desired.

Maggie came out of her fog to see her sister wearing a smirk and Lord Ravencroft with a firm grip on Crispin's shoulder. The earl's expression confused her. His frown held disapproval and a bit of anger. Why should he care if Crispin kissed her? He wasn't her brother, nor did they share a bond for him to feel as if he had to protect her. She still couldn't bring herself to call him Gregory, and his behavior only proved she had her reasons not to trust him. The kisses she shared with Crispin were none of his concern.

However, before Maggie could voice her opinion, Noel grabbed her hand and led them back to the house. She glanced over her shoulder to see Crispin growling at Ravencroft and twisting away from the earl's grasp. She tried to dig in her heels, but Noel kept them moving, muttering about Maggie's foolishness. Now Ravencroft and Crispin were arguing. Both of them thrashed their hands through the air in anger. They appeared to have the same mannerisms with each gesture they made. Which was ridiculous because they had never met until the Sinclair Ball.

Noel tsked. "You were lucky it was only Ravencroft and me who saw you two kissing."

Maggie rolled her eyes. "Please stop."

Noel continued with her lecture. "For shame, to kiss in such wanton disregard where Mama, Reese, or Graham might have come upon you."

Maggie latched onto a pole holding a lantern and forced them to a halt. She ripped herself out of her sister's grasp.

Noel tumbled forward but steadied herself before falling on her face. She turned around with her hands on her hips. "Was that necessary?"

Maggie growled. "As necessary as you found it to drag me away."

Noel shook her head. "Ravencroft thought it would be best to separate your embrace. Now come along, the gentlemen will return shortly. I am to make an excuse they are smoking cigars." Noel shuddered and then rattled on as usual, refusing to allow Maggie to defend herself. "I absolutely abhor those vile crutches, but Ravencroft enjoys them so. He has promised to only smoke them when I am not around. I'll make an exception this evening because we must cover up your foolishness."

Noel presented herself as an addlebrained twit who held no common sense. However Noel might portray herself falsely to society, Maggie knew her sister better than most. She wondered if Ravencroft realized her sister's true character yet or not. Maggie shook her head to clear out her thoughts about her sister. Another aspect her sister was excellent at, distracting one's thoughts from what they needed to focus on.

She observed Noel, recalling the comment she made. "Where else should I consider kissing Crispin? If not openly. Where do you and Ravencroft exchange kisses?"

Noel fluttered her hand at Maggie. "Exchange? We are not horses, dear sister. You do not exchange kisses but share them." Noel paused with a dreamy expression crossing over her features and sighed longingly. "Or they are stolen from you."

Maggie's eyes widened. "Stolen? Perhaps, *dear sister*, it is you who should explain yourself."

Noel drew her lips into a secretive smile. "Mmm." Noel never elaborated and sat on a bench nearby and patted the space next to her. "May I offer some advice?"

Maggie sat down and nodded for Noel to continue.

"Lord Dracott has only fallen back into Mama and Reese's good graces this evening. If you care to keep his standings the same, then you must not provoke them to change their minds again. And sharing kisses with him in the garden where anyone could see"—she pointed to the windows on the second floor—"would not be a wise choice."

Maggie closed her eyes, realizing her foolishness indeed. If Reese looked out his bedroom window, he would've seen the kisses Crispin teased from her lips.

She opened her eyes and nodded at Noel that she understood. "Thank you."

Noel smiled. "It is my pleasure. Now I only have one question before we make our return. Do Dracott's kisses make your toes curl? Because from where I watched, they made mine curl."

Maggie sighed. "Yes." She didn't care to know, but she must ask Noel the same question about Ravencroft. If Noel answered differently, then she stood correct that Ravencroft was not the gentleman for her sister. "Does Ravencroft's kisses hold the same effect on you?"

Noel rose and twirled in a circle. "And then some." With a wink, she skipped back inside.

Maggie smiled at her sister's silliness. She ran after her but paused before walking inside. She looked over her shoulder again; however, the gentlemen remained out of sight. With a shrug, she continued inside and sat next to Mama on the sofa.

"Did you have a pleasant stroll with Crispin?" Mama asked.

Maggie smoothed her hand along her skirts. "Yes, it was pleasant."

Mama frowned. "Did the gentlemen take their leave?"

Noel made their excuse for why they had returned without the gentlemen. "No. They are only smoking those atrocious cigars gentlemen prefer. Maggie and I preferred not to inhale the horrible scent."

"Bloody hell! Without me?" Graham stalked outside, making it clear whose company he would rather join.

Mama shook her head at his rude behavior. "Well, ladies, Graham shall see the gentlemen out. It is time for us to retire."

"But, Mama," Noel whined.

"No argument, my dear. We have an early morning appointment at the modiste for the final alterations on Maggie's debut gown and your wedding trousseau. I will not have you looking peaked."

Eden giggled.

Mama turned toward Eden and arched her eyebrow. "And what do you find so amusing?"

"How lucky I am not to be part of your visit to the dressmaker." Eden snickered.

"Oh, but you shall. You need to order a new dress for each event. Even Evelyn and Mina are coming along. We shall make it a Worthington ladies' affair."

Eden's groan caused Maggie and Noel to laugh at her misery. Mama rose, and they all followed her from the drawing room. They knew better than to argue with their mother once she stated her wishes. However, it didn't stop Maggie or Noel from glancing over their shoulders, hoping to catch one more glance of the gentleman they desired.

Unfortunately, they were out of luck.

Chapter Ten

RAVENCROFT THRUST A CIGAR in Dracott's face. "Here, smoke this." He lit the cigar and forced Dracott to inhale.

Dracott grimaced after taking a puff. "Must I?"

"Yes. Noel is informing her mother why we remain outside. I will not allow you to make a liar out of her," Ravencroft growled. "'Tis bad enough you mauled her sister."

Dracott's lips twisted. "Mauled? Why do you act like an uptight prude?"

Ravencroft threw his hands in the air. "I do not know where to begin with you. And we have little time. Once Noel returns and informs her family of the cigars we smoke, Worth will be upon us, wanting to join in."

Dracott flicked off the ashes, letting the cigar burn on its own. "Then let me make it simple. I will mention two names and we can start from there. If not, then we must meet later. The actions of others have forced us to make a plan to survive. If not, then your infatuation with Noel will crumble around you," Dracott threatened.

Ravencroft took a menacing step forward but stopped when he heard footsteps coming in their direction. "Who?"

"Ren," Dracott said. Ravencroft nodded since he had warned Dracott the night before of his friend's arrival. "Mother."

Ravencroft shook his head. "No. Mother would never return to Lady L's manipulations. We helped her to escape, and she made us a promise."

Dracott sighed. Even though Ravencroft was older than him, it was Dracott who held a jaded viewpoint toward people. Probably because he had had to endure more years of his mother's lies and betrayal to help her agenda. Ravencroft still lived in the idealistic period where his mother played at being a devoted wife and mother. Even year after year, when she betrayed him with her broken promises, Ravencroft still didn't grasp how evil their mother was.

"She offered Ren up as a sacrifice."

"Damn her." Ravencroft strode off to pace back and forth. "Where is she?"

Dracott shrugged. He wasn't able to gather any information from Ren. And when he tried to follow his friend, his search had turned cold.

"I wonder where your loyalties lie, Dracott. I thought you detested the act of smoking cigars," Worth drawled.

As Ravencroft cursed their mother, Dracott cursed Ravencroft. He had placed him in a predicament by making him smoke the cigar. Dracott had made his dislike for the nasty habit known one night while working late on a case. Ralston had bellowed his annoyance at Worth's inconsideration, and Worth had defended himself by declaring no clients wcre present, therefore he could smoke them how he pleased. Ralston had then enlisted Dracott's opinion, and he had stated how he detested smoking them. Hence why he held the cigar off to the side, letting it burn itself out.

"I forced him to, and of course, he objected. What gentleman does not like to inhale the smooth flavor of a quality cigar?" Ravencroft complained.

"Myself." Dracott put the cigar out, relieved he could stop the pretense.

"What do you say, gentlemen, shall we visit my club for a round of cards?" Worth asked.

"Sounds like a marvelous plan. The night is still young. Let me wish the ladies a good evening and I will meet you at your carriage," Ravencroft answered before striding away.

Worth quirked a brow at Dracott's answer. "Well?"

"I will pass. Today was long, and I must endure a longer one tomorrow. I have a task maker for an employer," Dracott quipped.

Worth laughed before taking a long drag on the cigar. "Did you have any luck with your search?"

Dracott shook his head. "Nay. She is a mysterious phantom. No one recalls seeing her."

"Were they all blind?" Worth demanded, distracted by the memory of the mysterious lady. "She was a vision who must have captured someone else's attention, as she did mine."

And she would remain so. Dracott already knew the lady's habits because he had taught them to her. The rest was her talent of blending in where needed while leaving her mark on those who served her purpose. And it would appear Worth was her intended mark.

"Does finding out her identity have anything to do with our case?" Dracott inquired.

"What?" Worth asked.

"The lady I am searching for. Is she involved with the case we are working on?"

"No. No. I just want to know her name."

"May I ask why?"

"Why?"

Dracott arched a brow. "That is what I am inquiring, too."

"'Tis personal," Worth muttered.

"Mmm. I understand." Dracott drew his hands behind his back, rocking on his heels.

Worth scoffed. "I highly doubt it."

"The lady holds your infatuation just as Maggie declared. And she has elusively escaped your clutches." Dracott smirked.

Worth leveled him with a glare. "Just find the chit," he demanded.

Dracott nodded. "Will do. Enjoy your game of cards. I will say good night to your family and make my way home."

"Do not come into the office until you obtain the information I require," Worth ordered.

Dracott chuckled, throwing over his shoulder, "It might take a few days."

He didn't wait to hear what Worth muttered. With Worth's order not to show his face, it allowed him more time to woo Maggie. He couldn't wait to make plans with her. Perhaps he would even climb on a horse and take a ride with her. It wasn't his favorite activity to partake in, but he would for her.

Dracott returned to the drawing room to find it empty, except for Rogers, who was locking the windows. "I am sorry, my lord. The ladies have retired for the evening. I shall see you out."

Dracott followed Rogers to the door, and the butler handed over his coat and hat. He didn't inquire about Ravencroft's whereabouts since he never passed him on the way out of the garden. No need to draw attention to his brother's activities.

"Thank you." He drew on his coat and placed his hat on his head.

"Have a good evening, my lord," Rogers said.

Dracott nodded his acceptance of Rogers's well-wishes. He took himself down the steps and into the darkness. He blended into the shadows as he made his way to his temporary residence. Dracott sensed someone following him. However, he held no clue who it might be. He knew he would find out soon enough because catastrophe would strike.

He only hoped Maggie stayed clear from the danger.

Maggie peeled her door open to make sure her path was clear. She inched out and crept along the hallway and down the stairs. With each step undetected, her nerves calmed. What she attempted should have set her nerves on edge, but it wasn't anything she hadn't attempted before. She had snuck out many times since they arrived in London. However, on this excursion, her family wouldn't consider her destination a safe place for a young lady to visit. On the other occasions, she only went as far as the mews in the alley behind their townhome, either to visit the horses or play cards with the stable hands.

Tonight, her destination would ruin her reputation forever if someone caught her. But it was a chance she was willing to take. She hadn't mistaken the passion held in Crispin's kiss this evening. It only left her to wonder what might happen if they were alone. Would his warm kisses involve soft caresses along her skin as he devoted himself to her pleasure? It only left Maggie curious about how he would pleasure her.

She didn't ponder the possibilities or else she would lose sight of him. Maggie ran along the soft grass to keep close to him but far enough away that he wouldn't see her. If he saw her, he would demand for her to turn around and return home.

Before she took another step, Graham's voice stopped her. "What took you so long?"

"I wanted to wish Noel pleasant dreams. But you know your sister, she kept rattling on," Ravencroft explained.

Graham laughed. "Should have known. Sorry, mate. We are under the impression she talks just to listen to herself."

Maggie frowned at Ravencroft's excuse. He had lied. They had taken to their bedchambers for the evening before Ravencroft's return. Maggie had listened for Noel's snoring to begin before she made her escape. Nor had she passed Ravencroft when she left. What was he about? The nagging sensation of how the gentleman was untrustworthy still sat with her. She must check with Crispin to see if he had learned anything about Ravencroft to verify her assumption for doubting the lord.

She peered through the bushes and saw Graham and Ravencroft enter the carriage. After they drove off, Maggie realized they had distracted her from following Crispin. It didn't matter though because she held a general idea of where Crispin's lodgings were. She had overheard Graham mentioning how they were behind the alley of their offices. She should find them simple enough.

"And where are we off to this evening, Lady Margaret? The mews are in the opposite direction," Rogers asked.

Maggie gasped. The butler had caught her stealing away into the night, and now her mother would send her back to Worthington Hall. When she first arrived in London, she had begged for that outcome. However, since she met Crispin, it was the last place she wanted to return to.

She slowly turned around. No excuses came to mind. "Umm."

Rogers arched an eyebrow. "Off to see Lord Dracott, are you?"

Her eyes widened in shock, and she nodded her head up and down.

Rogers regarded her with a shrewd gaze for an agonizing length of time before he shook his head. He took off, staying along the darkened path. When she didn't follow, he paused and turned back to her. "Hurry along." And he started off again.

After coming out of her shocked stupor, she no longer hesitated and caught up with Rogers. They walked for a while before Maggie attempted to understand the reason he offered to help. "Why are you helping me?"

"Do you not wish to spend some time alone with the young gentleman?"

"Very much so," Maggie whispered. "But it does not explain why you stayed silent about me sneaking out with Mama and Reese."

"It is my job to keep you safe. If I don't assist you, then you will find another way to visit Lord Dracott. One that would place you in danger," Rogers explained.

"Reese will end your employment," Maggie warned.

Rogers chuckled. "Rest assured, my lady, my position is safe."

Maggie pinched her lips. She didn't wish to argue with Rogers since he was helping her, but once her brother learned of this incident, they would both incur Reese's wrath.

Maggie made another attempt to understand this peculiar circumstance. "I suppose my actions do not bode well on my standing as a lady."

Rogers stopped them in their tracks. "Understand this, miss. In no way does this alter my opinion of you. You are a rare lady who approaches life differently from most, but it doesn't make you any less worthy. Lord Dracott is an upstanding gentleman and he will do right with you. That is my belief and nothing will change it. Do I make myself clear?"

"Yes."

He nodded, and they continued on until they reached a disheveled building. Boards covered the missing windows, and it appeared as if part of the roof was caved in. Crispin couldn't possibly live here.

"Where are we?" Maggie asked.

"His room is on the third floor, second door on the left," Rogers stated.

"But . . ."

"He works diligently for what he has. You must understand and accept Lord Dracott for the gentleman he is, not for what he doesn't have."

Maggie glanced back at the building. She had assumed since he was a viscount that he enjoyed the same privileges as her. It only went to show her how naïve and spoiled she was. Her family protected her from the harsh realities of life, and it gave her a sense of insecurity.

She came to visit Crispin for the selfish reason of her own pleasure. But now, she wanted to give Crispin the pleasure. She wanted to learn every facet of his character and what inspired him to act the gentleman he was today. After this evening, she would take nothing for granted again. Even the emotions Crispin stirred in her. She would leave him in no doubt of what she wished for them.

"You are not too bad yourself, Rogers."

Rogers chuckled. "Thank you, my lady. However, your time with Lord Dracott is slipping away if you are to return home before everyone awakens. I will continue to follow you until you enter his room. Do not leave this building unless Lord Dracott or I accompany you. Do you understand? There is danger lurking around every corner in this part of London."

Maggie nodded. She swiped her hands along the trousers she wore and then pulled the coat hiding her chest closer around her. She had worn a cap to hide her hair, hoping people would mistake her for a lad.

Once they reached Dracott's floor, Rogers nodded for her to proceed and signaled how he would wait in the dark corner. She took a deep breath and then tapped her knuckles against the weathered door. Her eyes darted everywhere, and her body twitched in fright at every little noise. When Crispin didn't answer, she knocked harder. Fear settled over her, urging her to leave. She was on the verge of running down the stairs when his door opened.

Although he only cracked the door, it settled Maggie's nerves. And the stormy expression in Crispin's gaze set her soul on fire. He didn't give her a chance to explain her arrival but wrapped his hand around her arm and dragged her through the door, slamming it shut behind them.

He pressed her against the door with a fierceness that should frighten her, but instead it heightened her arousal. With a swift tug, he flung the hat off her head, and her hair fell around her shoulders. A low growl vibrated from his chest, declaring every emotion pouring from his gaze.

"Maggie."

Chapter Eleven

CRISPIN DIDN'T KNOW WHETHER to strangle Maggie for her foolishness or kiss her luscious lips, which trembled from what could only be passion. Her eyes filled with a heat one only held when desire ruled their every decision. It had led Maggie to risk her life to come to his lodgings. Only the depraved walked the streets in this area of London. However, she hadn't made the trek on her own. He had seen Maggie arrive with Rogers from the window. He had sensed someone followed him home but hadn't expected it to be them, which only infuriated him more. What possessed Rogers to bring her to him?

He stepped closer to her with a fierce growl, hoping to scare her away. But she only raised her chin in defiance. His ability to refrain from kissing Maggie earlier had led them to this scandalous moment. He must send her away. Crispin was on the verge of succumbing to every temptation his thoughts clung to about her.

While he fought with his conscience, his body made its own decision. He wrapped his hand around her neck and tugged her into his arms. His lips swept down, leaving Maggie in no doubt of where the kiss would lead to. There was nothing gentle with his kiss. His fright over her well-being licked at his soul. He needed the ferocity of their embrace to help calm his scattered emotions. Crispin didn't know how to handle the vulnerability consuming him. Every emotion strung him in so many impossible directions. But with each sigh flowing from her lips, Maggie gifted him with a sense of security.

Maggie tasted the desperation in Crispin's kiss. He had fought to stay in control since her arrival. However, his kisses consumed her, tempting her to follow him wherever their passion may lead them. And follow him she would. She wrapped herself around him and clung to his frame while she met him kiss for kiss. His need didn't scare her away because her own need held the same fierceness.

Crispin reached down, lifted Maggie in the air, and wrapped her legs around his waist, pressing her up against the door. He tore his mouth away, and his fingers dug into her buttocks, leaving his mark as it burned through the coarse material. His lips trailed a path of fire along her neck.

"You are a foolish minx," Crispin growled near her ear.

Maggie threw her head back against the wall, savoring the caress of his lips. "As long as I am still a minx"—she sighed—"I do not care how foolish you may consider me to be."

Crispin pierced her with his gaze. "Why have you risked your life?" The rawness in his voice declared his fear.

Maggie's gaze softened, and she cupped his cheek. "Because I cannot stand to be apart from you."

Her gaze undid him. The fear for her welfare drifted away as he held her safely in his arms. Only his need to worship her with soft words, slow kisses, and gentle caresses replaced the unsettling emotion. He only wanted to lay her upon his bed, make sweet love to her, and listen to Maggie's sighs fill the air around them. He carried her to the bed and took her lips in the sweetest kiss he had ever shared with another soul. From this day forth, it would only be with Maggie.

There was no turning back.

He needed to love her. Her arrival was a gift he wouldn't refuse. He lifted his head and gazed at her body intertwined with his. Their clothing was an unwanted distraction. He wished her silken limbs were bare for him to gaze upon.

Maggie stared at Crispin through lids weighed heavy with her desire. His eyes raked her form. His bold stare seared a path from her toes to her chest, where his gaze lingered. However, he made no move to undress either of them. She worried he would change his mind, but his hand gliding gently across her stomach spoke otherwise. She ached to have his hand climb higher. With the brush of his lips against her breasts, they grew heavy with an ache only Crispin would ease.

Her nipples tightened at the very thought of Crispin ravishing her with his soft kisses. The pull of his lips on her nipples, circling them with gentle licks. Maggie whimpered her need. He must have understood her desperation because he untied the string holding the shirt together. With a swiftness that took her breath away, Crispin swept the shirt over her head and threw it across the room.

Crispin bent his head and drew a bud into his mouth, obeying Maggie's silent request. He sensed her need by her soft whimpers. He tightened his lips, sucking harder. Maggie arched her chest to his mouth, clutching at his hair and holding him at her breasts. He switched his attention to the other nipple, and her whimpers soon turned into sighs. Crispin eased her ache. However, he had only just begun to satisfy the need consuming them.

"You are a dream come true." Crispin raked his teeth across her nipple.

Maggie thought she would surely expire from Crispin's exquisite torture. When his hand slid between her thighs and rubbed against her ache, she wanted to crawl inside him. The need for him overwhelmed her. Her fingers dug into him when his strokes teased her, as did his mouth. She writhed around, pressing into his hand.

Crispin chuckled. "Easy, my love. We have only just begun."

His husky tease exploded in her ears, causing rippling tremors to overtake her. No longer did she lie there like an inexperienced lady unsure what to do. Instead she came alive, wanting to heighten Crispin's desire to the level he led her to. She wanted him to tremble with her and for them to join as one.

Maggie clawed at his clothing. Her impatient fingers pulled at his buttons, causing them to fly off the shirt. Crispin's amusement didn't deter her determination to feel his skin against hers. To have his hard body pressed into her softness. His chuckles vibrated against her stomach. He rose, straddling her body, and grinned down at her.

His hand trailed a path down her neck to cup her breast before moving across her stomach. "I should have known how wild you would be. You make love like you live life. Free. Wild. Uninhibited. Like a breath of fresh air."

Maggie couldn't speak. He stole her breath away with the wonderment in his tone. As if she granted him a special gift he felt unworthy of. She didn't understand why he held such beliefs and she had no words to offer him. Only her love.

Crispin slid back, slowly peeling away Maggie's trousers. He yanked off her boots and sent them sailing across the room along with her shirt. When he removed her pants, he brought them to his face. He closed his eyes and inhaled the sweet scent. He had imagined this moment since the first day he met her. The tantalizing memory kept him company on the long evenings he spent alone.

"These trousers have filled many fantasies," Crispin whispered.

"How so?"

"The very day I met you, I watched you ride away on your horse. Who knew a pair of trousers held the ability to make a man jealous? But I was because they hugged your arse like a tight glove." He chuckled. "I had to face the window for a length of time, so your family wouldn't notice the improper thoughts I held for you."

A warm blush spread across Maggie. The harsh red faded to a light pink the farther his gaze traveled along the length of her body. His gaze caused her to tremble in anticipation of his touch. He dropped the trousers and ran his hands along her legs, parting her thighs. Crispin wanted to touch his fingertips to her trembles and have them continue to spread throughout him.

"You fancied me then?" the minx teased him.

With a devilish grin, he slid a finger across her folds. At her gasp, her teasing smile disappeared, only for desire to spread across her face. With another stroke of his finger, her wetness coated him. He drew them to his mouth and sucked off the delectable juices.

"Ah, love, I believe I fancied you before I even met you," Crispin whispered.

He bent his head to savor what made Maggie so unique. Her sweetness coated his tongue with a flavor as exquisite as Maggie herself. Soon her sighs turned into moans as he pleasured her. Maggie was as free with her body as she was with her personality. His tongue pressed against her core, drawing out her desires to an unbearable ache he wanted to ease.

Maggie thrashed her head back and forth on the pillow in ecstasy. She grabbed onto the sheets, gripping them in her fists to keep from floating away. With each stroke of Crispin's tongue, she slipped further away. When his fingers slid in and out, pushing her need higher, she moaned his name over and over.

"Crispin. Crispin. Oh my, Crispin. Please," she whimpered.

She held no clue what she pleaded for, only she never wanted him to stop. Her pleas racked her body in a chant that only Crispin understood. He answered her mumblings with the gift of his mouth, offering her pleasure after pleasure. With her body strung tight and her toes the only part of her keeping her from falling off the ledge, Crispin blew a breath against her wetness. The soft caress sent her floating on the most wonderful sensation.

Crispin gathered Maggie in his arms, coaxing a kiss from her lips. She softened in his embrace, wrapping her arms around him in tenderness. Her hands fluttered against his chest in her attempt to show affection. Her innocent touch undid him and also inflamed his senses. He rolled her underneath him, brushing the hair away from her face. He lowered his head to place a kiss against her lips. However, Maggie returned his kiss with the fierceness of her desire, unleashing his need for them to join as one.

Maggie recovered from her floating, only to have her body scream its need to have Crispin fulfill her every desire. Her hands traveled over his body, curving and dipping into every muscle. He disguised his chiseled form behind his proper suits. Pure sin rippled over every inch of him. A blush warmed her cheeks at all the sinful ideas she wished to explore with Crispin under the bedsheets. With a kiss and the caress of his fingers, he turned her into a wanton creature.

Even now, with his desire pressed against her hip, he held himself back with the manners of a gentleman, but she only wanted him to unleash his passion and show her the depth of his desire. Perhaps with a little encouragement she could make him forget himself like she had forgotten herself.

Maggie's impish smile should have warned Crispin of her intent. Why he thought her innocence would keep her from acting improper was a foolish notion he held on to. He should have known better. He had lost his common sense once her hands struck their claim upon his person. Maggie's touch ignited a fire in him that turned into uncontrollable heat. Instead of it suffocating him, it only drew him closer to the flame for the full burn.

Her fingers dipped lower, brushing across his cock. A torturous moan slipped past his lips, causing Maggie's smile to turn into one only a vixen used to tempt a gentleman into her lair. However, Maggie didn't need to tempt. He gladly fell victim to her charms. When her hands wrapped around his cock and stroked him like a skilled courtesan, he almost came undone.

"How?" he croaked out.

Maggie chuckled seductively. "Graham has collected quite an assortment of wicked literature."

Crispin closed his eyes at her exquisite torture. Everything about her was exquisite this evening and only grew more exquisite. Her nibble fingers teased him. "I am sure he did not give you permission to look at them."

Maggie waited before answering Crispin. The hard steel in her hand distracted her from following the conversation. Her gaze kept drifting to watching his face relax in pleasure to clenching. The pressure of her grip determined which feature he gifted her. When his face clenched, he exhaled the most astounding moans that made her body ache for him again. Her nipples brushed across his chest, and she grew wet between her thighs.

"Mmm. No, he did not. One day, while I snooped for some chocolate he hid from me, I came across them. My curiosity got the better of me. They were very descriptive on how to give and receive pleasure."

Crispin growled his pleasure. "Grr."

She pressed her lips against his chest and trailed a path along his neck, her tongue striking out with soft licks. "Do I have the right of it?" Maggie whispered.

Her grip tightened, and Crispin thought he saw stars. He drew her hand away and held both of them above her head. His knee nudged her legs to open wider.

"Wrap them around my waist," he demanded.

Maggie obeyed his command. He grabbed his cock, and the warmth of her touch seeped into his fingers. With a gentle stroke, he ran it over her wetness, causing Maggie to arch into him. Soft moans echoed around them. Whether they were from Maggie or him, he held no clue.

Crispin's gaze pierced Maggie. "I cannot promise to be gentle, but I will try."

Maggie shook her head. "I want every ounce of your passion spiraling out of control inside me."

"I will not hurt you. However, you will experience soreness from your first time," Crispin rasped, holding onto his desire by a thin thread.

"I am not a fragile miss, Crispin. I know you will take gentle care of me. Please, do not hold yourself back from me. Unleash your passion on my soul," Maggie whispered her own demands.

Her soft touch against his heart was his demise. He pushed inside her as gently as he could but with enough force to lose themselves in the passion wrapping around them. Maggie held onto him as he pushed past her innocence. Her wetness clung to him like a vine, entwining him with her desire. She stiffened for a brief spell before she pressed up against him. Maggie commanded him to unleash the passion and give themselves over to one another. He granted her wish with slow gentle strokes. Each one built upon the last until he thrust into her with the power of their shared passion.

Once again Maggie floated; only this time Crispin floated with her while he wrapped her in his warm embrace. His mark would affect her for the rest of her life. Each time his body moved in sync with hers, his love entered her soul. Each time she thought her feet would touch the ground, Crispin shifted his position and sent them flying higher. His gaze alone seared itself into her memory, and she saw his vulnerability for the first time. She drew him to her for a kiss that held her promise to protect him as he protected her.

Maggie's tender kiss undid him. He unraveled into the man he wanted to be for her. He sent them over the edge with her tender lips soothing his battered soul. Maggie's affections made him whole again.

Crispin rolled Maggie over so that she lay spread across his chest. The wonderment shining from her eyes made him feel invincible. A dangerous emotion to hold, but one he would cherish while he held her. There was much he wanted to promise her, but he never believed in promises. They only held the heartache of broken excuses. However, it didn't stop him from telling her how much he cared.

"I believe I am falling in love with you."

Maggie pressed her finger against his lips. "Shh."

After they finished making love, Maggie saw the indecision in Crispin's gaze and realized Crispin carried a heavy burden. She didn't know what it was, but it troubled him. She also sensed he wasn't honest about the character he portrayed. He presented himself as an admirable gentleman, but there was more to him. Maggie would allow his secrets for a while. But soon he must confess his sins and only then would they confess their affections for one another.

Maggie wanted to avoid discussing their shared emotions, and he knew it was because of his dishonesty. He noticed how her gaze traveled around his lodgings and the quality of his possessions. She didn't question him, waiting for him to admit his failings. However, he couldn't yet. Not until Maggie was secure from the threat of Lady Langdale. He would stay silent because of his own selfishness.

To distract her, he slid his tongue across her finger and gazed upon her desire flaring to life again. He wished for nothing more than to spend the next few hours awakening her desires over and over again. But their time to depart drew near. Before long, he must escort Maggie home and hope no one learned of their indiscretion.

The familiar pull of desire sizzled around them. She might have just lost her innocence, but ever since she met Crispin, her body had reacted to his presence. Lying naked in his arms only intensified it. She moaned with longing, making Crispin's chest shake with amusement. She swatted at him.

"You, my lord, are a tease." Maggie pulled away, drawing the blanket around herself.

He folded his arms behind his head, smirking at her. "You have the nerve to call me a tease, my lady? When you sit upon my bed naked with only a sheet wrapped around you. A sheet that outlines your luscious curves."

She looked over her shoulder and cocked an eyebrow. "Yes. But you lie upon the bed unashamed in all your delectable glory."

He rose and brushed a kiss across Maggie's shoulder. "You find me delectable?" He nipped at her neck.

Maggie grew soft all over again at his lips upon her. Her body craved the satisfaction only his touch would grant her. Crispin's arm circled around her middle, bringing her back against his chest. He held her there, not saying a word, with his head on her shoulder. His warm breath washed over Maggie. His gesture meant more to her than what they had just shared. Not that she didn't love every minute of Crispin's lovemaking. But his affectionate gesture made her feel complete. Whole. Two soul mates treasuring their love.

"I must go," Maggie whispered.

"I know." Crispin hugged her tighter against him. He wasn't ready for her to leave, but he must release her so she could dress. With a soft kiss on top of her head, he withdrew his arms, and Maggie pulled the sheet around her. Her shyness after they made love was another adorable quality he enjoyed watching. A warm blush spread across her silken skin as she dressed. If he were a gentleman, he would turn his back and give her the privacy befitting a lady. However, as much as he tried to portray himself, he was no gentleman.

Crispin continued with his bold stare as she dressed. His intent was more than clear in how he wished for her to stay. He tempted Maggie to throw caution to the wind and join him under the covers for more lovemaking. However, common sense ruled her actions to finish dressing. She didn't want Crispin to suffer from Reese's or Graham's wrath for her boldness. He didn't sneak into her bedchamber to seduce her; instead she had stolen into his.

Crispin searched the room for his clothing once Maggie finished dressing. Maggie curled up into an armchair and returned his bold stare with her own. She sighed as she watched him pull on his trousers. It was a shame he had to cover himself. He was a fine specimen indeed. Most divine. Maggie giggled at the description.

Crispin raised his head. "What do you find amusing, minx?"

"Just a term Noel always used to describe a gentleman she was interested in before she met Ravencroft. And she still uses the word to this day. However, no other gentleman is as *divine* as Ravencroft. But I must disagree with her. For I find you the most *divine* gentleman I have ever met."

Crispin shook his head at her silliness. "Divine? And I had hoped you held a more masculine description of my appearance."

Maggie rose and glided over to Crispin, helping him to button his shirt. "Sorry, I forbid it."

"Oh, you do?"

"Yes."

"May I ask why?" He brought her fingers to his lips for a kiss.

"Because I want no other lady to realize what they are missing. If they were to whisper how brooding, strong, and sinful you are, then they would steal your attention away from me." Maggie pouted.

He lifted her chin with his knuckle. "Never fear, my love. No other lady will gain my attention because for our remaining days, I shall only focus it upon you."

A knock sounded on the door, and Rogers hissed behind the panel, "Dracott, you are pushing past the boundaries of my patience."

"You must leave, my love. When I arrive later today for a walk, we shall continue our discussion of how sinful you find me."

He never gave Maggie a chance to reply. Crispin gave her a kiss to remember for when she closed her eyes and fell into her dreams. It was a promise to the other kisses they would share again soon. He reluctantly pulled away and drew her toward the door.

Maggie's hand slipped from Crispin when she entered the hallway and Rogers greeted her with a frown. She had dallied with Crispin for longer than the butler had agreed to.

Rogers pushed her behind him and stepped close to Dracott. "Lord Dracott, I expect you to call on Lord Worthington at your earliest convenience," Rogers demanded.

Dracott leaned against the doorjamb with a cockiness he hadn't portrayed since he arrived in London. Hell, this sense of recklessness hadn't consumed him since his time on the Continent. However, after a few hours in Maggie's arms, his true self flickered to life.

He shrugged. "We shall see."

Rogers growled his distaste for the situation. When his glare didn't alter Dracott's stance, he stalked off. "We leave now, Lady Margaret."

Maggie hesitated, glancing back and forth between Crispin and Rogers. She didn't understand what had transpired between them since Rogers spoke so low. However, Crispin offered her a confident smile and tilted his head for her to follow Rogers. She had no choice because she must return home with haste. Soon, the sun would break through the darkness, and if she wasn't in her bed when that occurred, then she would face a doomed future with however Reese wanted to handle the situation. She took off after Rogers and didn't glance back once, because if she did, she would only run into Crispin's arms instead.

After they left, Dracott slipped back inside his room and tugged on his boots and overcoat. He glanced out the window and saw them walking toward the Worthingtons' townhome. On his way out, he grabbed a cap and slid it low over his head. Then he followed them, keeping back far enough to see them safely home.

Once they arrived, he waited around for a spell to stay close to Maggie. As he stood there, watching over the lady he loved, the eerie sense of someone following him settled over him once again. He searched his surroundings but saw nothing to concern himself over. Still, danger lurked nearby. A danger he couldn't prevent but would fight against with all his strength.

Maggie's love gave him the confidence he needed. While they never spoke the words, they didn't need to. The emotions that had shaken him during their lovemaking could only be the magic of love. While he thought love would overcome all of their obstacles, he wondered if Maggie would hold the same opinion once she learned the truth about him.

He hoped so.

Chapter Twelve

D RACOTT CRAWLED UNDER THE bedsheets, his body beyond exhausted. He desperately required a few hours of sleep before he gave his report to Worth. Unfortunately, he had nothing to report after spending the past few days searching for his friend. He couldn't give details on Sabrina's whereabouts, even if he had located her. She had hidden well. Which also left him unable to find Lady too. The case of Lady Langdale had frustrated Worth and Ralston.

He closed his eyes, but sleep eluded him. A tempting minx sprawled across him, and her teasing smile filled his thoughts. A smile he wanted to kiss from her lips. His body ached with his need for her. Not only his body but his heart, too. He hadn't seen her since their passionate night, which left him portrayed as a callous cad who had bedded her for his own selfish pleasure. He hoped his absence hadn't caused Maggie to doubt his intentions. If so, he would convince her otherwise, any way he could.

Just as thoughts of Maggie comforted him, the door to his room flew open. He jerked to a sitting position and reached for the knife he kept hidden under the pillow. At least he had had the sense to keep his trousers on when he laid down in bed. The door slammed shut behind the intruder, and Dracott relaxed when he saw Ravencroft.

"Where in the hell have you been?" Ravencroft hissed.

Dracott settled against the headboard, keeping a grip on the knife. "I did not know you cared so much for my welfare." Sarcasm filled his comment.

"Now is not the time for your wit."

Dracott sighed. He wasn't in the mood to deal with his brother. It only reminded him of the other problems he must deal with. "Then perhaps it is time for you to inform me of your plans. Or let me convince you to come clean with the Worthingtons."

"No!" Ravencroft snarled.

Dracott slid the knife back under the pillow and pulled on a shirt. After pouring them each a drink, he settled in the chair before the fireplace. Instead of sitting, Ravencroft threw back the drink and started pacing.

Before long, he stopped in front of Dracott and demanded again. "Well, where have you been? I had to listen to Noel complain about you all evening for abandoning your courtship of Lady Margaret. Then Worthington bent my ear for an hour about the doubts he holds about your character. You have placed me in a difficult position."

"Why? They are unaware of our relationship with one another."

Ravencroft sliced his hand through the air. "That is beside the point."

"Then what is the point?" Dracott asked.

"I need your help. Lady L has pushed the deadline forward. I have two days to supply her with the blueprints, and I cannot find where Worthington keeps them. I need you to help me draw up a rough sketch of the layout of their townhome. We have both visited the townhome enough to know the location of every room," Ravencroft explained.

Dracott sat forward. "No. I refuse to aid that bitch."

"You must. Margaret's life hangs in the balance."

Dracott sat back with confidence. "Maggie's safety is not an issue. I've arranged precautions in place to guarantee her protection."

"With Rogers?" Ravencroft scoffed.

Dracott didn't answer. Instead, he changed the subject. "Is Maggie well?" His brother stroked his curiosity with his comment about Noel's and Worthington's complaints.

Ravencroft plopped down on the chair. "Yes, she is well. Bored as usual with all the entertainments. Nothing too out of the ordinary. However, her gaze stays focused on every doorway with a longing glance, awaiting your arrival. However, you never show. Your absence causes her to refuse every offer to dance, leaving Lady Worthington in a snit."

Dracott swiped a hand along his face. He understood Lady Worthington's frustration quite well. "I will call upon the family tomorrow."

"And my problem?" Ravencroft asked.

Dracott rose and started toward the bed. "As I told you before, you are on your own. Now, if you don't mind, please see yourself out."

Dracott sighed in relief when he heard the door shut behind him. That was, until a familiar scent suffocated the air. He turned around and saw his mother wearing a smug expression.

"Mother," Dracott gritted out between his teeth.

Lady Ravencroft glided across the meager dwelling and bussed both of her sons across their cheek like a doting mother would do. However, his mother was far from what an affectionate mother acted like. No. She held the same traits as the evil woman she associated herself with.

"It is so wonderful our family is together once again." She made herself comfortable in the armchair and fluttered her hand toward the bottle of gin. "Gregory, be a dear and pour your mother a drink."

Ravencroft snarled his displeasure but did his mother's bidding. "What do we owe this pleasure, Mother?" Ravencroft delivered his own brand of sarcasm this time around.

Lady Ravencroft took a sip from the glass. "Is that any tone to take with your mother? I hope you do not speak to your intended in that respect."

Ravencroft never responded. He refused to mention Noel and give his mother an advantage over him. He folded his arms behind his back so she wouldn't see him clenching his hands into fists.

"I now see where you acquired the awful habit of not answering my questions," he muttered at Dracott. Dracott shrugged in response. "What do you want?" Ravencroft bit out.

Lady Ravencroft's chuckle bristled across her son's nerves. "Why, I miss my children."

Dracott scoffed, never offering his mother a word. He had learned early that his best defense was to stay silent around his mother. She could take the tiniest bit of knowledge and exploit it to her benefit. Her appearance back in their lives only proved her involvement with Lady Langdale. Now they must learn what part she played to stop her destruction. It would be no easy feat, but one he would enjoy while he sought his revenge.

He held no qualms about handing his own mother over to the proper authorities. She deserved worse, but he wouldn't waste his energy on the likes of her anymore. His only priority was Maggie.

"The truth, Mother," Ravencroft gritted out.

Both men gave her an unrelenting stare. Neither would accept her return with open arms. On that, they agreed. She had burned them more times than they could count, and neither of them trusted a single lie uttered from her lips.

Lady Ravencroft threw the drink back and rose to pour herself another. The dainty sip she'd taken before fooled no one. Their mother could drink a boat of sailors under the table. After she drank her second glass, she turned toward them with a calculating stare. When his mother held that look, it wouldn't bode well for any party involved.

"Very well. I heard the news that my eldest son is set to wed Lord Worthington's sister, and I wanted to offer my best wishes. 'Tis a shame he never told me of his wonderful engagement and I had to hear about it from the backhand gossip of a lady with a lower station than I."

"You hold no station," Ravencroft snarled.

"Oh, but I do. Your father never had our marriage dissolved. Therefore, I am still Lady Ravencroft," she gloated.

"A technicality. Your claim holds no standing in society. No one will accept your presence," Ravencroft declared.

Lady Ravencroft sashayed over to him and pretended to brush lint off Ravencroft's suit coat. "Oh, but they will when you present how much you accept my return. Also, I expect an invitation to the wedding. I am dying to meet my new daughter-in-law."

Ravencroft swatted her hand away before moving across the room. He needed space from his mother before she sank her claws in any deeper. "In which I have no plans to. Nor will I ever."

Lady Ravencroft made an irritating tsking noise. "You really have no choice but to."

Dracott watched his brother struggle to keep his temper in check and realized he must handle his mother. Ravencroft couldn't afford to have a scandal attached to his name or else Worthington would withdraw his support for the marriage. Dracott had witnessed their volatile relationship since he first met his brother. His mother always baited Ravencroft to lose his temper. To this day, he never understood why Ravencroft had searched for the mother who had abandoned him.

Not that Dracott wasn't grateful that he had. It was only with his brother's support that he had escaped his mother's hold. Ravencroft showed him how another world existed outside the hellish existence he lived in. He must set aside his own trepidations and deal with their mother. The sooner they dealt with her, the sooner she would disappear from their life again.

Dracott sighed. "Say what you have to say, Mother."

Lady Ravencroft twirled around to face Dracott. "Ahh, he speaks." She walked toward him and patted his cheek. "I have missed you so."

Her need to constantly touch him whenever she was near annoyed him. He gritted his teeth. "Answer Ravencroft," Dracott demanded.

Lady Ravencroft tugged on her gloves. "You two are such spoilsports. How is a mother to enjoy herself when her sons will not play along?"

He drew in a breath to help calm his impatience. "You know very well polite society will not accept you into their fold. It does not matter if Ravencroft escorts you himself to his wedding. Everyone in attendance will give you the cut direct."

A cunning smile lit Lady Ravencroft's face. "Then you both must convince Lord Worthington about how I wish to make amends."

"Never!" Ravencroft growled.

"Never is such a harsh declaration, my dear," Lady Ravencroft drawled. "It is in your best interest to at least attempt a reconciliation. If not, how will your behavior appear to Lady Noel? You do not want her to believe you are a heartless scoundrel who turns his back on his less fortunate mother. Do you?"

"Leave Lady Noel out of this," Ravencroft ordered.

"Ahh. Do you care for the lady? I never imagined it to be so. Well, this changes everything."

Dracott shot Ravencroft a warning to keep his mouth closed before Ravencroft walked right into their mother's trap. "Mother, shall we get to the reason for your visit?"

"I already told you how I wish to be a part of my son's life. I have seen the error of my ways and wish to repent." Lady Ravencroft's voice softened as she told her lie.

"Pure shite," Ravencroft snarled.

They were getting nowhere. His mother would never admit to why she was here. She played a part and wouldn't break out of character. The only way she would leave was if they consented to her wish. "All right. Ravencroft will make the introductions soon. In the meantime, perhaps you should remain keeping a low profile until it is safe."

"Like hell!" Ravencroft thundered.

"Safe?" Lady Ravencroft questioned with a look of innocence.

Dracott held out his hands for them both to hear him out. "If mother attempts to enter society again, then you must portray a united front. If not, Lady Noel will suffer the consequences of rejection more than either of you will." Dracott focused on his mother. "You cannot show yourself until we clear your name. You are on a list associated with Lady Langdale. It states how you are one of her accomplices. Until then your safety is at risk."

Dracott watched his mother's confident smirk turn to fear and couldn't help himself. "I do not think you will fare well in Newgate. Do you, Ravencroft?"

Ravencroft chuckled at Dracott's barb. "No, I do not believe so."

Lady Ravencroft stomped her foot. "You two are impossible, not to mention cruel. What children find humor in their mother's demise?"

Dracott shrugged. "Children who had to endure a lifetime of hell with you as their mother."

She advanced on Dracott with her fist held back, ready to strike him. At one time, he would have cowered from her brutality. But with Ravencroft's help, he had learned how to defend himself. And Maggie's love had given him the confidence to endure any battle set before him. When he didn't even flinch, she lowered her arm.

"Ahh, I see the wench restored your confidence once you bedded her. However, I wonder how she would feel about you if she knew the truth of your identity." She glanced between her sons. "I take it neither lady is aware of how you two are brothers."

When they both stayed silent, they supplied their mother with the answer to her suspicion. "When will either of you learn? Stick to the truth as close as you can while working a con. Because the truth will always come forth. Your deceit will only make for some uncomfortable dinner conversations. Not unless you do not plan to make an honest lady of Lady Margaret. Was she only a replacement for your precious Ren?" Lady Ravencroft snarled in distaste.

"What in the hell is she talking about?" Ravencroft demanded.

Lady Ravencroft waved her hand in the air. "Oh, you know how your brother has an affliction for ladies who wear breeches."

"Tell me you did not bed Lady Margaret," Ravencroft pleaded with Dracott.

Lady Ravencroft chuckled. "Well, she was in his lodgings for a considerable amount of time, leaving one to speculate on their activities. Also, there was Rogers's threat to Crispin to call on Lord Worthington the next day. But he never called." She appeared quite pleased with herself and continued. "How is Rogers these days? You must send him my regards. I do miss his company."

Dracott needed his mother to leave before Ravencroft unleashed his fury on him. He never planned for his brother to learn of his indiscretion with Maggie. "Where are you staying?"

"With a friend," Lady Ravencroft answered.

"If the friend is Lady Langdale, I insist you break your ties. The only way for us to clear your name is to prove your innocence, and if you continue hiding out with her, then it only shows proof of your guilt," Dracott explained.

Lady Ravencroft rolled her eyes. "Very well. I must complete this assignment for her and then I am free to go. Gregory, your time to supply the blueprints is running out. She expects them by tomorrow evening. Any attempt to thwart her plans will end in your dcmise. She will provide the authorities with proof of your involvement in her thievery ring. Then she will expose Crispin for who he is. Lady L will strike her revenge while the Worthington family suffers from the shock of your betrayal."

Lady Ravencroft walked to the door. She had accomplished what she had set out to do. She left behind destruction as she always did, forcing her sons to pick up the pieces.

However, before she left, Dracott needed one more piece of information from her. "Ren?"

She turned and arched an eyebrow. "What of her?"

"What is her role?"

His mother looked at him with sympathy. "Her attachment and deception go far beyond what you believe of her. I warned you about her. Maybe one day you will heed those warnings, before she destroys you."

With those last words, she left. Tension filled the air from her visit. His brother stood glaring at him, waiting for an explanation. However, he must follow his mother instead of soothing his brother's battered ego. She would lead him to Lady L and hopefully Ren, too.

He grabbed his cap and set off. His brother ran after him, grabbing his arm to spin him around.

"You bedded her," Ravencroft hissed.

"Shh." He pressed Ravencroft against the wall when he heard his mother's footsteps pause on the steps. Once she started again, he turned to Ravencroft, holding a finger to his lips. "Later," he whispered.

Ravencroft snarled but nodded in acceptance. They kept to the shadows as they crept down the stairs, listening to their mother inform the carriage driver of her destination. Once the carriage took off, Ravencroft pointed to his carriage waiting for him across the street. They ran to it, and he ordered his driver to follow the other carriage but keep at a distance to stay undetected.

His brother glared at him while they rode along. He didn't need to listen to Ravencroft's lecture to understand his disappointment. Usually he held remorse for his actions, but in this he held none. He didn't regret the magical evening he'd had with Maggie. He only wished to share many more with her.

"We will discuss this in depth later," Ravencroft ordered.

Dracott shrugged. "We shall see."

"That is not for you to decide," Ravencroft declared before the carriage jerked to a stop, sending them colliding against one another.

Dracott glanced behind the curtain to notice his mother entering a prestigious residence in Mayfair. He quirked a brow at Ravencroft in question at who owned the home. Ravencroft shook his head. It didn't matter. Now he could restart the investigation Worth and Ralston had come to a standstill on.

"We must confess our deceit to the Worthingtons. There is no other way to stop our mother and Lady Langdale," Dracott whispered.

"No. Give me another day. I will come up with a plan," Ravencroft insisted.

Dracott stared at his brother and listened to the desperation in his voice. He owed it to Ravencroft to figure something out. His brother had saved his life on more than one occasion and rescued him from their mother's clutches. He owed his devotion to Ravencroft foremost. But he also recognized the madness of the situation and needed to make his brother see reason.

"One more day," Dracott offered. And nothing more.

Ravencroft nodded his head with determination. However, Dracott didn't know if determination would be enough.

"Now spill," Ravencroft demanded.

Dracott noticed movement and saw Ren stealing away. She moved from bush to bush with stealth like he had taught her. He knew if he followed his mother, he would find Ren.

"Later," Dracott said as he slipped out of the carriage.

"Dracott," Ravencroft growled.

But Dracott had moved away too swiftly for Ravencroft to catch him. He blended into the shadows and tracked his friend. She kept glancing behind her, but he stayed hidden from her view. When she rounded a corner, he followed, only to find she had disappeared on him. He slowly spun in a circle, but there was nothing but complete darkness. She had led him into an alley with no light shining from anywhere.

Uneasiness settled over him. In his haste to follow his mother, he had left home without a weapon. Now he stood unprotected, a defenseless animal waiting for a predator to attack. It shouldn't have surprised him when someone swept his legs out from underneath him.

He landed on the ground with his assailant leaning over him, holding a knife to his throat. The techniques Ravencroft had taught him vanished from his thoughts, and a panic he couldn't control set in. In his attempt to control his breathing, it only intensified his fear. Sounds echoed in the distance, and a flashback from his past consumed him.

Blackness surrounded his vision, and he fell into the deep hell his mind delivered him to.

Chapter Thirteen

MAGGIE SAT IN THE drawing room with her family and their guests. Mama had invited Evelyn's family to join them for dinner. However, only a few of them had accepted the invitation. The Duke of Colebourne sat on the sofa between her mother and Evelyn, talking about their favorite subject, Mina. He liked for everyone, including Maggie, to call him Uncle Theo. Evelyn's cousin, Gemma, who was also married to Graham's business partner, Ralston, sat talking with Noel about her upcoming nuptials. They were the best of friends. In the corner, Evelyn's twin sister, Charlie, and her husband, Jasper Sinclair, debated with Reese on the merits of good horseflesh.

Usually, Maggie would have joined their discussion. However, her heart rejected the polite atmosphere for the evening. Maggie had worried over Crispin's welfare since she hadn't heard from him for a few days. She had overheard their whispers about his absence from the office and how they had received no messages explaining his whereabouts. When she questioned them, they placated her with false smiles, pleading his absence on a case. The same excuse Graham made to Reese for why Crispin never called on her. Graham promised Reese that once they finished their case, he would give Crispin leave to court Maggie to Reese's satisfaction. Graham's comment only provoked Reese and made him more difficult to deal with.

Maggie didn't know what to make of his disappearance. Every day, he had sent tokens to express his regrets for his absence since their passionate night together. However, nothing had arrived today. Had something happened to him? What case sent him into hiding? Most of their cases revolved around finding a missing object and only required obtaining a confession. Never anything dangerous.

Maggie's curiosity grew once Eden joined their conversation, and she saw how serious their expressions turned. What were they involved in? And was Crispin in danger? Maggie grew more worried when Eden offered her a sympathetic look.

Then there was the matter of Ravencroft. His attention this evening made her uncomfortable. His gaze upon her held many questions. It was as if he tried to understand her character. His stare was upon her every time she glanced up from her plate. He watched her as if she held all the answers to his questions. Which only led her to wonder what those questions were. Had he played a part in Crispin's disappearance? She had seen them arguing in the garden the other evening. Had Crispin learned something nefarious about the earl and Ravencroft sought to keep him silent?

She narrowed her gaze at him, and instead of glancing away, he returned her stare. For a second, she could've sworn she saw desperation and an indescribable emotion hidden in his depths, which was foolish. Wasn't it? When she glanced back at him, he had moved on to join Graham, Ralston, and Eden. They stopped their discussion and teased Ravencroft about his upcoming nuptials.

Ravencroft acted like a swell sport, taking their ribbing like a pro. His pensive mood changed to one of a love-stricken groom. Maggie rolled her eyes. He laid it on a little too thick. Didn't anyone else notice his false character? He had her entire family fooled. While Reese pondered Crispin's character, he should focus his attention on Ravencroft before Noel walked down the aisle. It didn't seem fair. Reese faulted Crispin for acting like an upstanding fellow who came by his wealth honestly. Unlike Ravencroft, who waited for a payout once he spoke his vows with Noel. Instead of forging his own path in life, Ravencroft waited for her brother's handout. And for that, Reese was misguided with his acceptance.

"Well, Meredith, shall I help you make a match this season for young Maggie?" Colebourne winked at Maggie.

Colebourne's exuberance and love for matchmaking brought a smile to Maggie's lips. A few years ago, he had made matches for his entire family. Even Evelyn and Reese's marriage had resulted from Colebourne's hijinks. It was a well-known tale amongst their families.

"There is no need, Uncle Theo. I have already made a match of my own," Maggie replied.

Colebourne chuckled. "Oh, indeed? I must hear the details."

"Perhaps if the bloke would ever pay a call on Maggie, we could elaborate. For now, we shall not speak of the courtship," Reese declared.

Evelyn shot her husband a warning glare, but it was her mother who came to Crispin's defense. "Lord Dracott is courting Maggie. He is a viscount who works alongside Graham and Ralston. We were hoping he would join us this evening so you could meet him. However, Graham has Lord Dracott working on a case."

Colebourne's eyebrows drew together. "Dracott? His name sounds familiar, yet I cannot place him. It will come to me.

It must be an important case to keep him away from the company of young Maggie."

Graham cleared his throat, appearing uncomfortable with the line of questioning. "Yes. But one we should finish soon."

"I would love to learn more about it. Perhaps I will call on your office tomorrow. Gemma has told me of your success of late." Colebourne praised Graham and Ralston.

Soon, Colebourne shifted the discussion onto Noel about her wedding. The duke always tried to make everyone feel appreciated and that he cared for them. When Reese and Evelyn married, their two families had become one. They were a tight-knit bunch with Colebourne holding court in the center.

Mama offered her a smile of support. She knew how much Maggie had been missing Crispin. While her mother never voiced another objection to Crispin's behavior, she disliked seeing Maggie upset. Mama even stepped in when Reese voiced his dislike for the situation.

Maggie's gaze drifted around the room to the harsh whispering between Graham and Ralston again and their panicked expressions when they glanced at Reese and Colebourne. Maggie suspected the case they worked on had ties to the two gentlemen, which only spiked her curiosity to learn more. Perhaps she should attempt to sneak away again this evening. She would wait until Rogers was asleep since she had memorized the path to Crispin's place. Perhaps she would find her answers there.

During her musings, she missed Ravencroft leaving the drawing room. She wondered where he went, but her thoughts over Crispin's welfare consumed her, and she soon forgot about her sister's fiancé.

"If everyone will excuse me. I want to peek in on Mina before calling it a night. I enjoyed everyone's company this evening.

With any luck, you can meet Lord Dracott during our next *family* dinner."

While Maggie spoke to the room at large, Reese was the one she focused her direction on. Her brother quirked his brow at her boldness, but Maggie only offered him a sweet smile. He shook his head at her, biting back his own smile. Her declaration spoke of her affections for Crispin being a part of their lives and her brother answered her with his reluctant acceptance. His response satisfied her.

After everyone wished her a good evening, Maggie walked to the nursery. She stood in the door, watching her niece sleep, clutching her favorite doll. She was such a sweet child. The complete opposite of Maggie, but she adored her more than anyone else. Everyone adored Mina. She had everyone wrapped around her little finger. She was simplicity. Innocence. A joy brought into their family that had at one time suffered uncertainties.

Mama had always brought light into their life and made their home peaceful and loving. However, whenever Papa visited, he had only brought darkness with him. After he left, they had struggled to fall back into their normal routine, only to have him wreak havoc on them once again on his next return. Maggie never told a soul, but when her father died, she had suffered no remorse for his passing. Everyone had thought they kept the ugliness hidden from her, but she had seen through the drama for what it was. A soulless man who tortured his family with his cruelness.

After their father's death, Reese had adapted to their father's nefarious habits. But it was with Evelyn's love he had broken free from the chains holding him down. She saw the same determination in Crispin's eyes, how he tried to escape from a darkness known only to him. She wanted to help guide him into the light. Maggie wished Reese would understand how

Crispin fought his own demons. He was a good man, the only man for her.

Maggie couldn't help herself. She stepped inside and placed a kiss on Mina's cheek. "Sweet dreams, little one."

She continued to her bedchamber, only to find Evelyn, Charlie, and Gemma inside. Evelyn and Gemma watched Charlie with amusement as she dug through Maggie's wardrobe.

"And here I thought nobody else was as disorganized as myself. But this girl is a mess. Now, where does she keep her breeches?" Charlie mumbled.

Evelyn chuckled. "Probably somewhere Mama cannot find them."

Maggie interrupted. "Hence it being a hiding place."

Charlie tilted her head to the side. After staring at Maggie for a few seconds, she pointed at the bed.

Maggie shrugged at how it might be the hiding spot. However, Charlie smirked and shook her head that it wasn't. She circled the room, and soon a smile lit her face. Charlie pulled open the bottom drawer of a chest ladies used to keep their sewing in. After rummaging around to the bottom, Charlie pulled out a stack of clothing, comprising of her breeches and one of Graham's old shirts. The same garments she had worn the last time she snuck out to see Crispin.

Maggie quirked an eyebrow at Charlie. "Has Sinclair taken away your breeches, so you think to steal mine?"

Charlie waggled her eyebrows. "No. He quite enjoys it when I wear breeches. Oh, the stories I could tell you of how much he enjoys them."

"Charlie!" Evelyn warned.

"What? We are attempting to help the girl sneak out. Why must you censure me?"

Evelyn stuck out her tongue. "You are incorrigible."

Charlie smiled. "Yet you love me all the same."

Evelyn sighed. "That I do."

Charlie threw the clothes at Maggie. "Hurry and change. We have little time."

"Little time for what?" Maggie asked.

Charlie motioned her hands for Maggie to obey her command. She moved to the doorway, watching the hallway for anyone to disturb them.

Gemma took pity on Maggie's confusion. "Because we are going to help you see Lord Dracott."

Maggie turned a questioning stare at Evelyn, and her sister-in-law nodded. "Why?"

"Why else? You miss him. It is more than obvious. Your brother and Ralston have kept him away because of a secret case. We notice your doubt and want to help ease your worries," Gemma explained.

"You would help me and endure Reese's wrath if he were to find out?" Maggie asked.

Evelyn held an impish smile. "Leave your brother to me. No one will even realize you are gone. Trust us."

Maggie needed no other reason because it didn't matter anyhow. She had planned to see Crispin after everyone retired for the night. Who was she to pass up any kind of help? Their offer kept her from the danger of making the trek all alone in the dark.

She changed her clothes, pulled up her hair, and hid the tresses inside a hat. Once again, Maggie disguised herself as a young lad. Then she stood with her hands on her hips, facing her co-conspirators. "Now what?"

"Now you sneak into Gemma's carriage and wait for us," Charlie instructed.

"What about Ralston?"

"The gentlemen have decided to join Uncle Theo at his club for a game of cards. With some encouragement, they were more than eager," Gemma explained.

"All right." Maggie moved toward the door, then stopped. "I do not know how to express my gratitude."

Evelyn rose and gathered Maggie's hands into hers. "There is nothing for you to say. Us ladies must stick together in the matter of love."

"We understand the misery of being separated from the one you love. You are worried about what keeps you apart," Gemma added.

Charlie laughed. "Plus we love scandal."

The other ladies shared secretive smiles. Maggie understood what those smiles meant. They were expressions of how they had each risked ruination to spend time in their lover's arms. Maggie felt honored they included her in their pack, considering her youth. But then again, age didn't matter with love.

Their support empowered Maggie to tell Crispin of her love for him and convince him to tell her his secrets. She wished her sisters were as supportive, but she understood why they weren't here. Noel would never attempt to defy the rules, no matter how much Ravencroft tempted her. But then Ravencroft left Noel with no doubt of his devotion. Eden treated Maggie like a child at times and expressed a mother's affection. Also, Evelyn was just as much of a sister to her.

"Thank you then."

Charlie shooed her out the door. "Hurry. We shall be along shortly."

After hugging Evelyn, Maggie slipped down the servant's staircase and made her way to the mews. She waited until the driver climbed aboard before she slipped inside the carriage. Maggie drew her knees underneath her, trying to stay undetected. When the carriage stopped in front of the townhome, Maggie never moved an inch.

"Franks, please take us around to Lord Dracott's lodgings. Lady Worthington was kind enough to prepare a basket for his dinner," Gemma directed.

Franks cleared his throat, looking uneasy. "My lady, please allow me to deliver you home first. 'Tis not a proper section of town for ladies to travel through at night."

"Nonsense. It shall not take long," Gemma insisted.

"Very well, my lady," Franks conceded.

Maggie understood the fellow's predicament. It was useless to argue with a Holbrooke lady. They were a formidable force you could never win against. It was far easier to admit defeat and follow their wishes.

Charlie and Gemma settled on the seats, wearing grins at how they executed their plan with precision. Their satisfaction was infectious, and soon Maggie smiled with her own enjoyment.

Gemma explained their plan. "Now, when we stop at Lord Dracott's lodgings, we will disembark first, pretending we will deliver the basket. As we distract the driver, you slip out and pretend to come from across the street."

"Then you shall pretend you are Lord Dracott's servant and we will pass the basket off to you," Charlie finished.

Both ladies sat across from Maggie, impressed with themselves. Maggie wished it was as simple as they proposed. Even though she planned to visit Dracott on her own, her doubts still plagued her. Would he get upset that she had shown up unannounced? What if he entertained another lady? No. She must stop thinking the worst. She trusted Crispin, and she refused to allow her foolish thoughts to convince her otherwise.

When the carriage slowed, Gemma glanced out the window. She turned to Maggie with a frown. "I am not sure we should stop."

"What nonsense. Why ever not?" Charlie asked.

Gemma nodded out the window. Maggie understood Gemma's hesitation because she had held the same opinion on her first visit to Crispin's lodgings. She remained quiet. It didn't matter because Maggie would still visit Crispin this evening.

Charlie peered around Gemma and grimaced. "Perhaps you are correct. Evelyn will never forgive us if we leave Maggie alone here."

Gemma pondered over Dracott's situation. "I thought Lord Dracott resided in better lodgings. His clothing is impeccable, and he carries himself with pride. I am sure Ralston pays him handsomely, too."

Maggie repeated Rogers's comment. "He works hard for everything he has, and that is all you need to understand and accept."

Charlie sat back in her seat, impressed by Maggie's affirmation. "Still, it is not wise of us to leave you here."

Maggie sat forward and reached for the door handle. "Either way, I will see Crispin this evening."

"Stubborn, just like her brother," Charlie muttered. Charlie pretended a dislike for Reese because of the time he tried to pursue her when Evelyn loved him. Maggie always found the story humorous. Reese still managed to irritate Charlie, and after each occasion, the friction started all over again. It appeared Maggie reminded Charlie of Reese at this moment.

Once Gemma realized Maggie wouldn't bend, she swatted Maggie's hand away. "All right. But you must send us a signal once you reach his room so that we know you are safe. Or else we are following you inside."

Maggie nodded vigorously.

A knock sounded on the carriage door. "Lady Ralston, we have arrived. If you hand over the basket, the footman will deliver it, and we can be on our way." Franks's voice quivered.

Gemma signaled for their ploy to begin, and Maggie leaned back. Gemma shoved the basket out the door and into the servant's waiting hands. Then the two ladies disembarked with the flurry of their skirts, and they caused the distraction needed for Maggie to sneak out. Charlie motioned behind her back for Maggie to move into position.

"Perhaps I should deliver the basket and inquire about Lord Dracott's welfare," Gemma said.

"An excellent idea, cousin," Charlie agreed.

Maggie scrambled out of the carriage and snuck around the rear, keeping unnoticed by the footmen. They stood next to the driver, guarding Gemma and Charlie, and attempted to dissuade them from entering the lodging rooms.

"'Tis not proper, my lady. Nor is it safe." Franks attempted to convince Gemma of the logic of the situation.

Maggie shuffled by them with her hands in her pockets. She made it past them, ready to enter the building, when Gemma spoke out. "Boy! Are you not Lord Dracott's servant?"

Maggie turned, keeping her head low. She feared the servants would notice her since she had spent time in the stables. "Yes, my lady."

"Excellent. Would you be so kind to deliver this basket to Lord Dracott? Tell him it is from Lady Worthington, and she sends her regards," Gemma explained.

Maggie stepped forward and grabbed the basket. "Will do, my lady."

Gemma pressed a small bag of coins into Maggie's hand. "For my gratitude." Then she whispered low enough for

Maggie to hear, "Take a hackney home. Do not wander these streets alone."

"Thank you, Lady Ralston," Maggie grumbled.

Maggie rushed inside, relieved to have gotten this far. She hurried up the stairs and almost knocked on Crispin's door but stopped when she heard arguing voices behind the panel.

She pressed herself around the corner and waited for the visitors to leave. As she waited, Maggie remembered the promise she had made to Charlie and Gemma to reassure them that she had arrived upstairs safely. She slid the basket against the wall and hurried to the window. She sent them a signal, and soon the carriage took off. Maggie barely made it back to her hiding spot when Crispin's door opened. She stood in shock when Rogers and a young lad strolled out. They closed the door and continued their discussion in hushed whispers.

Maggie almost stepped forward to confront Rogers when the door opened again, and Ravencroft stalked outside. She gasped at the fury on his face and pressed herself against the wall. Their conversation drifted around the corner to her.

"What happened?" Ravencroft demanded.

Maggie chanced another peek around the corner.

"He passed out when I attacked him," the lad mumbled.

"Attacked him? Are you a fool?" Ravencroft roared.

Rogers glanced around them, expecting the other tenants to open their doors. "Ren only meant to scare him," Rogers tried to calm Ravencroft.

Ravencroft advanced on the lad, pulling him up by the scruff of his shirt. He dangled the boy in the air. "Why did you have to return? We helped you to escape. You were free."

The lad spat in Ravencroft's face. "Free. I will never be free. Plus, you only have your mother to blame for my return."

Mother? Maggie thought Ravencroft's mother had passed away years ago. She swore she had overheard him telling Noel the sad story of her demise. Maggie knew a scandal revolved around his mother, but she couldn't recall the exact details of the lady's fall from grace.

Ravencroft snarled. "So your loyalties lie with that bitch again. Was it your intent to kill him?"

Rogers pulled at Ravencroft's arm to lower the boy. "Let us discuss this in a more private setting." He nodded toward the closed door. "We all have the same intention toward him, and arguing over his welfare is not helping matters."

Ravencroft dumped the lad on the floor. "Just explain how you attacked him."

The lad pushed himself to his feet. "I swept his feet out from underneath him and pulled a knife to his throat. I did not know he still suffered from his terrors."

Ravencroft growled, grabbing for the boy again. The boy sidestepped Ravencroft, but not before Ravencroft grabbed the lad's hat. Only it was no lad. A luxurious mane of hair the color of a raven fell from atop her head and hung past her shoulders. *Who was this creature?* And how did she have intimate knowledge about Crispin? She obviously knew more about him than Maggie did.

Ravencroft sighed. "When Dracott becomes stressed, his terrors escalate out of his control."

Rogers attempted to get them to leave again. "We need to leave. It is not safe for any of us to be seen together."

"Fine. We shall finish this discussion in my carriage," Ravencroft ordered.

He stalked away, and Rogers followed him, but the girl hesitated, placing her hand on the door. Her look held concern and something more Maggie didn't want to understand.

"Ren!" Ravencroft hissed.

Rogers moved back and pulled the girl from the door. "He will be fine. I gave him a sedative to help him sleep."

"Should someone not stay with him?" she insisted.

"No. We cannot risk it," Rogers explained.

Rogers helped the girl along the hallway and down the stairs. However, she kept her gaze focused on the door until she moved out of sight. Who was she? More importantly, how were Ravencroft, Rogers, and the young girl connected to Crispin? Ravencroft acted protective of Crispin, which made no sense at all. She had told Crispin of her doubts about the earl, and Crispin had assured her he would look into Ravencroft. Was it a cover to hide their relationship?

The longer Maggie stood in the hallway, the more she risked getting caught. Once she realized they wouldn't return, she rushed to the door and turned the knob. In Ravencroft's haste to confront Rogers and the girl, he had neglected to lock Crispin's door. While it benefited Maggie, she had to wonder if he had done so on purpose. And if so, why?

Maggie opened the door, eager to discover what ailed Crispin. Only, when she stepped inside, nothing could've ever prepared her for what she met. She opened her mouth to scream, but no sound poured from her lips.

The man before her wasn't who she fell in love with, but a man set out to protect himself. The far-off gaze in his eyes scared Maggie more than the knife raised above his head, ready to attack. His gaze reflected the depths of a lost, frightened boy who lived in a hell he was unable to escape from.

Maggie's heart cried out at Crispin's vulnerability. How had she missed seeing this side of him? What terrors had he endured in his lifetime to leave him in this state?

"Crispin?" Maggie whispered, stepping forward. She held her palms out in front of her to show she meant no harm. She approached Crispin with the same calmness she had of the frightened horses she worked with.

Her calm voice offered him reassurances of her intention toward him. He wasn't himself at this moment, but a shell of a victim set to protect himself at all costs. When she reached out to touch him, he recoiled, jumping away from her. Maggie kept talking. When she stepped forward again, he backed away, shaking his head. When they were close to the wall, she stopped. She didn't want him to feel trapped.

"Crispin, my love. It is Maggie."

A heart-wrenching moan tore from Crispin's throat, and he advanced on her like a predator, but Maggie stood her ground. She pleaded with him to break the hold from where his mind wandered.

"Crispin. Crispin. Crispin," Maggie repeated.

He towered above her, his knife inches from her heart.

"I love you, Crispin." The words trembled from Maggie's lips.

She might have sounded confident, but she was anything but. His actions terrified her, but her feelings for Crispin stood firm.

His hand lowered, and Maggie clenched her eyes shut.

Waiting.

Chapter Fourteen

THE KNIFE CLATTERED TO the floor at their feet. Crispin stared down at Maggie in horror. When she opened her eyes, the fear pouring from them stabbed him in the heart. However, the fear vanished, and sympathy wrapped around him. He gathered Maggie in his arms and held her close to his heart. Trembles racked his body, but they weren't all from him. They sank to the floor as their emotions overcame them.

Maggie lifted her head, and Crispin plundered her lips. He drank from them in his desperation to forget what he had almost done to her. His lips begged for forgiveness, while his tongue stroked against hers with dangerous intent. Maggie clung to him, her kisses making her own demands that Crispin met with each pull of their lips. He should pull away from her and demand that she leave. She wasn't safe with him. But he couldn't release her from his arms. Maggie was his salvation. The need coursing through him was more powerful than anything he had felt before.

Flashbacks from his past clawed and dug into the sweet harmony surrounding them. He refused to allow them to inflict harm. Maggie was too pure for him, but he needed her to survive. He fought his demons with each kiss and caress upon Maggie. He tore off her cap and threaded his hands into her hair, devouring her lips with a need he couldn't control.

Maggie gasped at the intense desire circling them. Crispin's lips trailed a path of danger along her neck, branding her with his need. Each little nip pressed harder against her skin. She wanted to soothe him. However, he entrapped her in his desperate passion, and her body begged for release.

They tore at each other's clothing in between their fiery kisses. Each caress grew bolder than the one before. Crispin worshipped Maggie's body, drawing out her passionate cries. Her lingering moans and soft sighs soothed his battered soul. Her fingernails digging into his back heightened his need to make her his again. And her kisses gave him proof of the salvation he reached when he held her in his arms.

He rose, picked up Maggie, and carried her to the bed. While he acted like an animal with his scattered emotions, he wasn't a brute to take her on the floor.

Maggie writhed underneath Crispin. Her need grew uncontrollable. "Crispin," she whimpered.

Crispin paused, staring at her with a crazed expression. Unlike the one before, this one informed Maggie how he meant to fulfill every desire she held. His stormy gaze held hers, while his hand brushed across her core. Her whimpering turned into a torturous moan. His eyes narrowed as if he hoped for a different reaction. Then he slid two fingers inside her. Her wet channel guided them in smoothly, and he started a rhythm of movement, strumming her body with his touch.

"Ahh." Maggie's eyelids fluttered closed at the exquisite sensation.

"Open your eyes," Crispin demanded.

She slowly dragged her eyes open, and Crispin's stare dominated her senses. They blazed with the victory of pleasing her, yet she also noted the determination to possess her soul. Maggie was at his mercy to do whatever he pleased. She welcomed him into her heart, and it was only right for him to have her soul, too.

"I love you, Crispin," Maggie whispered.

Crispin moaned. "Ah, love."

Her declaration pierced through years of feeling unloved and unwanted. The desperation that overcame him when he realized he had almost killed her washed away. He only wanted to love her as gently as he could. She deserved nothing less. However, as much as he wanted to worship her with soft kisses and caresses, his body demanded to fill her and make them one.

Maggie noted how her words calmed him. His touch grew soft, and his features settled in peace. When he slid inside her, it wasn't with a force to forget his demons, but with a gentleness of a man who loved the woman he claimed. Each stroke spoke of his devotion to her. Each slow, agonizing movement sparked a flame of desire filled with an everlasting emotion shared only between them.

Crispin laced their hands together and bent his head to brush whisper-soft kisses across Maggie's lips. Their bodies moved as one. Their legs entwined, and Crispin's chest brushed across Maggie's breasts, causing the friction to intensify with each movement. Maggie whimpered again when Crispin pushed in deeper and settled without moving. She pushed her hips against his, desperate for him to move. However, he stayed still. Her wetness gripped his cock, clinging with her need. Her fingers tightened around his. Each time her hips pressed tighter, he clung to his control.

He waited.

When one lived in hell their entire life, they only wished to savor heaven for as long as they could. Maggie was his heaven. Her body was the temple he wished to worship every day for the rest of his life. He planned to pledge his devotions to her daily.

However, for now, he only wished to express three simple words he had never spoken to another soul before. "I love you."

Crispin's devotion ripped from his soul in a raw voice as he soared into Maggie. Each stroke drove deeper and deeper, with Maggie melting underneath him. He unraveled around her, and Maggie caught him in her embrace. He clung to her in the aftermath of their passion. Her soothing words seeped into his conscience, and tears slid down his cheeks.

She never asked why he cried. She only dried his tears and kept whispering her love for him. He closed his eyes, fighting against the pull of sleep, but the lingering effects of the sedative dragged him back under. He would only rest for a minute. Then he would explain to Maggie his lies and the deceit that followed in his wake.

Maggie continued to hold Crispin close to her heart while he slept. His tears had long dried, but the proof still lay heavy in Maggie's heart. They were a symbol of the demons he held onto. She wanted to fight every single one of them until they declared defeat. Now, she only needed to learn what they were.

She never imagined her evening would end in such a dramatic conclusion. When she set out, it had been to visit with Crispin, and instead she had witnessed a conspiracy with a mysterious girl, Rogers, and Ravencroft. She had gained no answers from Crispin. As she came upon him, he had come at her with a knife in a confused state, then he made love to her in a way that kept her heart skipping a beat. It had started intensely and ended in sweet torture.

When Crispin remained sleeping, not even rousing when she moved, Maggie realized their discussion would have to wait. She heard the carts moving on the streets below. Soon the vendors would sell their wares, and Maggie would miss her chance to sneak home undetected. She tiptoed across the room and dressed.

"Maggie," Crispin murmured.

Maggie glanced over her shoulder to see he had only talked in his sleep. A smile crept across her face. He thought of her, even in his dreams. His action assured Maggie that all would be well. She returned to his side and stared down at Crispin while he slept. She bent over, brushed his hair from his eyes, and placed a soft kiss against his lips.

"We shall talk later, my love."

Maggie hadn't even taken a step toward the door when it flung open. She gasped and searched for the knife Crispin had dropped. She didn't even notice who the intruder was. Maggie saw the knife, ran to pick it up, and turned, ready to defend herself.

Ravencroft held his hands up. "Put down the knife, Maggie."

Maggie shook her head. "No."

Ravencroft stayed still. A lady with a knife was a dangerous individual, and he had already had his share for the evening. Maggie glared at him. He glanced around the room and noted his brother was still in bed. However, his clothes lay across the floor and Maggie held Crispin's knife. What had happened? He hoped his brother hadn't attacked Maggie. However, it would explain her defensive behavior.

"I mean you no harm," Ravencroft tried to reassure her.

She pointed the knife at Crispin. "But you cannot speak the same for Crispin," Maggie accused.

A look of concern crossed Ravencroft's features. "Did Crispin harm you?"

Maggie recoiled. "Your question is absurd!"

Ravencroft nodded toward the clothes on the floor. "Is it?"

Maggie blushed a fiery red. "Stop distracting me. Why are you here?"

Ravencroft winced at the change of the uncomfortable conversation. By the color of Maggie's cheeks, he spoke out of line. It would appear his brother and his fiancée's sister had shared an intimate moment, which would explain why she stood in defense. She thought to protect Crispin from him. The thought comforted him. Crispin needed more people in his life to show him his worthiness in receiving love.

"I came back to check on Crispin," Ravencroft explained.

Maggie's face scrunched in confusion. "Crispin? You say his name as if you share a closeness."

Ravencroft sighed. Crispin was right. They needed to confess their deception. This evening proved how dangerous it was for them to accomplish their revenge on their own. They were no match for Lady Langdale and the destruction she hoped to attempt.

"Because we do. He is my brother."

Maggie took a step back, unsure how to respond. 'Twas impossible. "No."

Ravencroft took a seat to show Maggie he wasn't a threat. "Yes. We share the same mother."

"Impossible. Your mother is dead."

Ravencroft scoffed. "If only that were so. It would make life a lot less complicated."

"How so?"

Ravencroft quirked a brow. "I do not believe you need me to explain how that is possible."

Maggie cleared her throat and avoided Ravencroft's gaze. "Not that. Explain how the circumstances came to be."

"'Tis not my story to tell. I only told you of our relationship for you to understand that I mean him no harm."

Maggie glanced between Crispin and Ravencroft, deciding if he told the truth. She would prefer to hear Crispin's explanation. Still, she needed her questions answered. "Who was the girl from earlier?"

Ravencroft dragged a hand down his face. A complicated question that, if not answered correctly, could affect the result of Maggie forgiving Crispin once he told her the full brunt of the truth about who he was. "They are friends, nothing more but nothing less."

Maggie peered at him with skepticism. "Your answer makes no sense."

"Another topic best answered by Crispin since I do not understand the depth of the friendship myself."

"And Rogers?"

"A friend as well."

"Someone else Crispin will need to explain?" Maggie asked. Ravencroft nodded.

Maggie turned her attention to the bed and studied Crispin. While the two gentlemen held no apparent similarities, Maggie noted how they shared a likeness. Perhaps she had never noticed them before because of her dislike for Ravencroft or her infatuation with Crispin.

"We actually share the same hair color. He puts dye in his hair to cover the difference. If not, his natural color showcases our similarities," Ravencroft pointed out.

Maggie kept staring at Crispin. His dishonesty didn't alter how she felt about him. She knew he held secrets by the way he carried himself. After this evening, she realized he carried a heavy burden with those secrets.

"We should leave before your family discovers your disappearance." Ravencroft rose and started toward the door.

"Will he be all right if we leave him alone?" Maggie whispered. Her concern for Crispin grew when he never awakened during their conversation.

"Yes. He only needs to sleep off the sedative I gave him earlier."

"Why did you give him a sedative?"

"It helps him overcome his terrors."

"Terrors?"

Ravencroft walked over to Maggie and peeled the knife from her hand. He slid it under the pillow next to Crispin, the place where his brother hid the weapon. Then he gathered Maggie's hands into his. "Crispin has lived a life of hell until recently. The guidance he has received from Worth and the love you have freely given him has been the perfect tonic for his soul. I only wish I could have given him half of what your family has. But that is my grievance to bear. I only ask for you to keep an open mind when he confesses his sins. Give him the patience he will need to overcome his demons."

Maggie tilted her head as she listened to the sincerity in Ravencroft's words. She had misjudged him, which left her wondering about his intentions toward Noel. "Do you play Noel false? Or do you care for her as greatly as you do Crispin?"

Ravencroft squeezed her hands. "When I love someone, I love them with my entire heart and soul." He turned and walked to the door.

"Do you love Noel?"

Ravencroft paused. The question was one he didn't wish to consider at this moment. It held its own complications. "A matter I will only discuss with your sister."

"Fair enough," Maggie replied.

With one last lingering glance at Crispin, she followed Ravencroft into the hallway. She watched him lock the door behind him. Maggie wanted to berate him for neglecting to protect Crispin earlier, but it would get them nowhere. She also wanted to question why he held a key to the lodging, but it was likely because Crispin had given him the key.

During the carriage ride, neither of them spoke. They were both too deep into their thoughts. Also, they had nothing left to discuss. Ravencroft had made it clear Crispin must answer her questions and his relationship with Noel was none of her concern. When he spoke so passionately about how he loved, it had left her to question his devotion to Noel. While she found fault with it before, she now believed the earl cared for her sister. Only time would tell.

When they arrived behind the townhome in the mews, he stepped down and helped her out. Then he followed her through the garden to make sure she entered the townhome safely.

"I only ask one favor of you, Lady Margaret."

"And that is?"

Ravencroft folded his hands behind his back. "For your silence on my relationship with Dracott. There are powers at play you are unaware of. Dangerous individuals who mean harm to those who you and I both love. And until I can secure the safety of Dracott and myself, then I must have your promise to stay silent."

Maggie struggled with his request. She never kept secrets from her family other than sneaking out to see Crispin. However, what Ravencroft asked of her was monumental. Also, she realized the dangerous elements he mentioned in Crispin's behavior and also the night she had spied Ravencroft speaking to a lady in the woods.

"I will only stay silent until I can talk with Crispin. Moving forward from there will depend on what Crispin and I decide together. However, we will warn you about our decision. In the meantime, no harm comes to the ones we love," Maggie declared.

"Fair enough," he answered before sauntering away.

Maggie watched Ravencroft leave, more confused than ever. She had never imagined the evening she just endured. But it was one she would remember to her dying day. Crispin had declared his love for her, not only with his words but with his soul.

A declaration given freely and one that would secure a lifetime of never-ending devotion from her.

Chapter Fifteen

D RACOTT WOKE WITH A start, his breath coming out in quick gasps. The lingering effect of his nightmare clung to his consciousness. His gaze scanned the room for any sign of a threat, and he relaxed once he realized he was alone.

He slid back against the headboard and propped his arm on his raised knee. His head lowered as he attempted to recall the fragments of his nightmare. He wanted to discern the horrible sense of doom settling over him.

The glint of the silver blade peeking out from underneath the pillow drew his attention. He sat up straighter, peering around the room again.

Dracott threw the pillow off the bed and saw how the blade faced the wrong direction. He always placed the knife with the blade facing toward the headboard. A flashback of him holding the knife over an intruder invaded his thoughts. The weapon beckoned him to tap into his memories. Dracott picked up the knife and shut his eyes to concentrate.

Flashes of getting attacked mixed with him grabbing the knife because someone had invaded his lodgings. Also, memories of making love to Maggie mixed in with his terrors, distracting him. However, the image of Maggie standing before him with a look of horror etched on her face brought the evening slamming back.

He dropped the knife and leapt from the bed, backing away at the memory of attacking Maggie. He bumped into the table and knocked the bottle of gin and glasses around. With an unsteady hand, he reached out to grab the bottle. The liquid burned a path of fire down his throat to settle in his belly. He kept drinking after the first swallow didn't appease his remorse.

"Maggie," Dracott croaked out a whisper.

Still, images of them declaring their love while their bodies moved as one continued to plague him. Her soft confession whispered in the air.

I love you.

The memories seemed so real. They weren't figments of his imagination. Or were they?

He took a deep breath to help calm his troubled thoughts. Panicking wouldn't solve the doubts plaguing him. Only clear thoughts would help him reach clarity. And getting drunk because of acts he had committed wouldn't help him absolve himself. He must piece together what he remembered and hope everything else fell into place. This wasn't the first episode of forgetfulness he suffered from, nor would it be his last. How he conducted his mindset, though, would put his doubts into perspective.

Dracott noted the disheveled bed, his clothes strewn across the floor, a chair pulled close to the bed. A glass of water with a bottle of sedatives sat on the nightstand, and a blanket hung over the curtains, keeping out the light. Those small touches meant Ravencroft had been present. Only his brother knew how to handle one of his episodes. As frustrating as Ravencroft had been of late, he held gratitude for his care.

With one more glance, he memorized how the room appeared and closed his eyes. After taking a few deep breaths, he cleared his mind to focus on the events from the night before. A short time later, piece by piece came together. He worked on staying calm, even during the memory that triggered his attack.

He remembered he had spotted Ren and fled Ravencroft's carriage to catch up with her. However, she had led him into a darkened alley. He had had no way to protect himself since he had foolishly left home without a weapon. Someone had attacked him, throwing him to the ground. Not realizing it was Ren who swept his feet out from underneath him, he had flashed back to the memory of when he received a brutal beating during a heist gone wrong. Dracott had stared into Ren's eyes, noting it was her. But he had still grown confused and passed out, a reaction he succumbed to whenever he felt threatened.

He dragged a hand down his face. By now, he had come to terms with his unmanly reaction. As much as he wished he wasn't so vulnerable, it was something out of his control. His best course of action was to never place himself in those situations. And working for a detective agency wasn't the wisest of choices for an occupation.

While he didn't recall how he had returned to his lodgings, it must be the work of Ren and Ravencroft. As much as his friend didn't trust his brother, she did if it concerned his welfare. By the room's appearance, his brother had helped to ease his trauma. Usually, he only needed to sleep off the effects of the episode.

However, he recalled waking up in a groggy haze and hearing someone enter his room. He had reacted from instinct and drawn his weapon to defend himself. But in his confusion, he had mistaken Maggie for an intruder. He recalled how Maggie had attempted to make him see reason, but he had mistaken her actions as a threat. Bits of her pleas tugged at his memories.

His body shook at how close he had come to causing her harm. However, it was her declaration of love that had awakened him out of the fog he had existed in. Soon, every memory rushed forward in a flood of images. The kisses they shared. The ever-consuming passion exploding around them. Her gentle caresses and soft sighs of pleasure. The exact moment when their souls joined to create an everlasting bond of love.

Maggie's gentle embrace as she held him to her heart while he cried out from the agony of the demons that clung to him, even with her gift of love surrounding them. Maybe together they could free him from the claws of his demons.

After that, he had fallen into a deep sleep. The full effect of the drug had taken over him.

He opened his eyes after he remembered everything. Shame never once took hold because he realized it was an uncontrollable wasted emotion. His behavior was an act he accepted, and if Maggie loved him, then she needed to understand it, too. And her reaction showed him she did.

Now he must confess his other sins and explain what had happened. And to do that, he must betray Ravencroft. Which was for the best. His brother's insane plan to outwit Lady L was an impossible feat, one thcy would need the aid of more powerful gentlemen to complete.

Dracott rose and put his chamber in order. After dressing, he set out. First, he would pay a visit to Maggie. She deserved his attention before anyone else. He only hoped she would listen to his confession and forgive him afterward. Then with her support, he would confess to Worth and Ralston and ask for their help. If neither gentleman called him out, he would then ask Lord Worthington for Maggie's hand in marriage. He only prayed the earl would agree. If not, then he might have to kidnap Maggie.

A smirk settled over his face as he contemplated how that plan might work more to his advantage.

More thrilling, at least.

Maggie never slept. Sleep eluded her because of her scattered emotions. After tossing and turning, she finally rose and dressed for the day. She stayed in her room, not wanting to appear too eager for breakfast. She knew in her heart Crispin would call on her this morning. If she sat waiting for him, she knew Evelyn wouldn't stay silent. And it was for the best that her brothers never discovered how she had snuck out to visit Crispin. They would beat him to an inch of his life, drawing out his misery with their overprotectiveness.

Then there was Ravencroft. He always joined them for breakfast, and now they shared secrets between them. Secrets Maggie herself didn't understand. However, it wasn't fair to keep these secrets from Noel. While she had told her fair share of fibs, she never withheld information from her family. She hated betraying Noel. But she must stay silent until she spoke to Crispin first.

Maggie curled up on the divan and stared outside. The staff were pruning the flowers, and the gardener chased a cat away. Maggie giggled. Her heart sat heavy from her memories of the previous evening, but the amusing sight gave a lift of lightness to the doom. Not every memory was unsettling. She clung to Crispin's words of love and hope for the outcome of their deception.

They had much to discuss, but she held confidence they would conquer the obstacles in their path. It wouldn't be easy, but together they would succeed. She must rein in her patience before she unraveled from the uncertainty. To help calm herself, she closed her eyes and brought forth the memory of their lovemaking.

Crispin's desire for her held an intensity brought on by his attack. However, Maggie had never once felt an ounce of fear toward him. Her soul cried at what he might have endured in his past, and her soul rejoiced at every emotion he brought forth with each caress he brushed across her skin. Each of his kisses spoke of his possession of her heart. Her fingers trembled across her lips as she traced them. The intensity of his kisses awakened her senses even now.

Maggie laid her head on her folded arms and watched the sky grow brighter from the rising sun. Her eyes drifted close, and she dragged them back open. She didn't want to fall asleep and miss Crispin's visit. However, exhaustion took hold and she succumbed to her body's need to sleep.

No matter how much she resisted otherwise.

With his thoughts focused on his explanation to Maggie, Dracott was oblivious to the carriage following him. A sense of danger gripped him as he crossed through the park to reach the Worthington townhome. He tipped his hat at a couple passing him before glancing over his shoulder. A carriage with a suit of arms had stopped a few yards behind him. However, the carriage disappeared once he reached the gate leading out of the park.

Dracott walked to the corner of the street. Before he could take another step, the carriage pulled in front of him. Two burly footmen grabbed him and threw him into the carriage. They left him with no opportunity to resist. Dracott landed on the floor and slammed his head against the door. He kept his head lowered, not wanting the person who had grabbed him to find pleasure in his discomfort.

She was the root of his nightmare. The terror who haunted him with her demands. However, she wasn't alone. He should've known his mother would turn against them. Her visit to his lodgings was nothing more than a warning, one they had failed to respond to. Now, he must deal with the consequences of his mother's betrayal. Lady L had made her return, and now she would extract payment from everyone she controlled.

He pushed himself to the opposite seat before addressing them. "Mother."

The other lady raised an eyebrow in disapproval at his rudeness. Instead of responding, he crossed his arms in front of his chest and waited for the lady to state her demands. He knew his insolence would irritate her enough to lose control of her temper. He played a dangerous game, but one he must, to protect those he loved.

Instead of stroking her anger, his silence only seemed to amuse her. "Yes. There is a difference with the boy." She made a tsking noise. "How the love of a simple girl makes a boy brave. 'Tis a sad act to watch."

Dracott gritted his teeth, refraining from taking her bait. "What do I owe this displeasure?"

The lady shook her head in disappointment. "And he has lost his sense of respect. But what do you expect when he has fallen for a hoyden? I can see where her lack of manners has rubbed off."

Dracott employed the techniques Ravencroft had taught him to keep his temper under control. He counted to ten, but instead of a calm approach, he only wanted to strike out with his own insults. Maggie was ten times more of a lady than the one before him. Lady Langdale was gutter swine. She might have married into the aristocracy, but she held less worth than the whores who worked in the East End.

His nostrils flared, and he tightened his hands into fists at his side. He must remain calm or else she would feed him to her goons. He couldn't afford to suffer another relapse because no one held a clue of his whereabouts to help him.

"Have you guessed why I have asked you to join me?"

Dracott scoffed. "Asked?"

The lady laughed. "I quite enjoy the man you have grown into. No wonder young Maggie has fallen so hard. Though I much prefer your hair in its natural state." She fluttered her hand at his head. "This color is atrocious."

"I tried telling him," Lady Ravencroft added.

"Yes, he is obviously a man who has reached a point where he no longer listens to his mother's advice. If he had, we wouldn't find ourselves in the predicament we are in now. Would we?"

"Barbara . . ." Lady Ravencroft started.

Lady L growled. "Do not say my name aloud."

Dracott chuckled. "Do you imagine you fool anyone? Soon everyone in London will learn of your arrival and you will find no hole large enough to hide under."

Lady L pulled off her gloves. "One should not sound so cocky unless they have proof to back up their words."

Dracott relaxed back in the seat. "I need no proof. You are a wanted lady and will soon meet your demise."

"Ah, that is where you are ahead of yourself, *Lord Dracott*. What a horrid name and disguise. However, it no longer matters. This morning your employers will receive an anonymous tip and proof about how you are a member of Lady Langdale's thievery ring. This will, therefore, end your

LAURA A. BARNES

position with Graham Worthington and Barrett Ralston. Also, my past lover, Reese Worthington, will receive a letter."

"What did you do?" Dracott snarled.

"Why, your mother sent Reese a letter explaining your identity and the different scams you ran throughout England and on the Continent. As a fellow peer, she refused to condone your actions in pursuing his sister and ruining her virtue. Even though the ton no longer accepts her anymore, she didn't want Ravencroft's chances with Lady Noel ruined," Lady L explained.

Dracott sat forward in his seat. "You had no right."

Lady L laughed. "When will you ever learn?" She sat forward to where they were only a breath apart, and she spoke with menace. "I own you."

Dracott had never wanted to strike a lady before. But Lady Langdale was no lady; she was a vindictive shrew. He never understood what any gentleman saw in her. They were always too blinded by the act she performed.

Lady L looked out the window before addressing him. "Now onto business. Your brother's deadline has expired. He failed to supply me with the drawings I requested. His defiance has resulted in my need to destroy both of you. Not only for disobeying my instructions, but for helping Sabrina escape. Thanks to your mother, Sabrina has returned so that I may watch over her welfare. However, it doesn't lessen my annoyance at her disappearance."

The carriage slowed and pulled off the path of the road. Dracott realized they had left the city and what awaited him when he stepped from the carriage. Lady L would set her goons upon him to beat him to within an inch of his life. She wouldn't allow them to kill him. No. She would enjoy the entertainment of how he would suffer from their abuse, then take pleasure from the shame she set into motion.

Maggie would learn the truth of his deception at the hands of Barbara Langdale. A truth, no matter who delivered it, would hold the same effect. Only his description would have held his personal agony. Either way, the Worthingtons would learn of his twisted involvement and how he had tried to cover his tracks. He hoped the love Maggie expressed would help her understand the reasons for his deceit. If not, then the hell from his past would consume him again.

Dracott had no words for either lady because they were cut from the same cloth. Their only agenda was for themselves. His mother may have given birth to him, but that was as far as her motherly care extended.

He opened the door and stepped out of the carriage to his doom.

Maggie had overslept, missing breakfast. And Crispin. Her family had left the dining area, and the servants had cleared away breakfast. Should she wait for Crispin to pay a visit or should she make an excuse to visit Graham's office?

The house held an eerie sense of silence. Maggie wandered from room to room, deciding on her next course of action. Where was everyone? The parlors and library sat empty, and when she looked outside, she noticed a light rain fell. So they wouldn't have taken a walk in the garden. Maggie climbed the stairs and looked in her sisters' chambers and couldn't find them. Even Reese and Evelyn's bedchamber door remained closed.

And she had learned early in their marriage to never disturb them. She smiled, now understanding why. When she was younger, she'd had the tendency to walk in on them during some intimate moments.

Since she couldn't find Mama, Maggie figured Noel had talked their mother into another shopping excursion. She shuddered at the thought. One highlight, at least from oversleeping. She had hoped to ask Eden if she had seen Crispin since Eden worked alongside Graham on a few cases. Perhaps Eden held some insight into his character she hadn't noticed. Not that she doubted him. She only wished to learn everything about him. She wanted to understand what had traumatized him.

Maggie lingered in the hallway, unsure what to do. She heard the silly giggles of her niece and went to play with her. In the meantime, Maggie hoped someone would return home or else Crispin would pay a call.

She stood above Mina. "Are you being silly, Miss Mina?" Maggie tried to talk in a stern voice but only ended up giggling herself.

Mina clapped her hands. "Play, Mags. Play."

Maggie laughed at her enthusiasm and dropped to the floor. "What shall we play?"

"Dolls and teatime," Mina stated to her aunt as though it should have been obvious.

Maggie cringed when Mina selected her dolls and set them around the small table. Even as a child, Maggie had never played with dolls. She had preferred the outdoors and horses. Even now, she longed for the open fields and the babbling brook on their estate. She wondered if Crispin enjoyed the outdoors or if he preferred the city more. They had much to learn about the other.

"Mags." Mina patted the chair next to her.

Maggie joined her niece for playtime with dolls and tea. She would indulge Mina the same way her family always indulged her when she was younger and preferred playing in the barn.

"Who do we have joining us today?" Maggie asked, glancing around the table.

Mina made the introductions in a grown-up voice, pulling another smile from Maggie's lips. While she enjoyed the morning with her niece, she realized her troubles would work themselves out, and all would be well.

It had to.

Chapter Sixteen

"WHERE IN THE HELL is Dracott?" Ralston demanded, pacing across the office.

Eden noted her brother's sheepish expression while he tried to make excuses for Dracott's absence. What fool errand did Graham have Dracott chasing after? Probably the name of some light skirt. Her brother was hopeless. However, his excuses only made Ralston grow more impatient with the delay.

Lord Falcone had arrived with pertinent news that required immediate attention. Her gaze shifted to the arrogant lord. He sat with a smug expression, displaying his pride at the information he delivered on breaking the case concerning the whereabouts of Lady Langdale. Before long, he would gloat over his discovery. Her dislike for the gentleman grew each time she came into contact with him. Which, unfortunately, happened more times than she had liked lately.

She had held dislike for the marquess since the first time she met him during her stay at the Duke of Colebourne's estate. He had attempted to draw a wedge in between her friends Jacqueline Holbrooke and Griffen Kincaid's courtship by slandering the viscount with false accusations. However, his actions had held no effect on their courtship. They were happily married with a child and another on the way. However, the tension between the two gentlemen continued, especially when they needed to join forces with Kincaid's security firm. As they needed to for this case.

Her gaze strayed toward Lord Kincaid, who had propped himself against the wall, waiting for their meeting to begin. Kincaid stayed quiet and ignored the marquess, making everyone aware he only held contempt for Falcone.

This investigation had taken a chaotic turn, and if no one brought it under control, they would lose their chance at capturing Lady Langdale and her crew.

Eden rose, walked over to Falcone, and knocked his feet off the desk. Besides annoying her with his presence alone, she found him to have the manners of a brutish oaf. Falcone's reaction only fueled her annoyance when he smirked at her. If it was only a smirk, she could respond with a sarcastic remark. However, he raked his gaze over her body with a slowness that one would only describe as slow perusal. The bold stare left her flustered, and for a brief second, he made her forget her purpose.

Oh, yes. Chaos. She must start the meeting and not dwell on Falcone's agenda, for whatever it was, it would only end in trouble.

She knocked on the desk, drawing their attention toward her. "Gentlemen, we need to begin. We can inform Lord Dracott of our news when he arrives." She shot a glare at her brother for the delay.

Worth gave his sister an innocent smile in his attempt to rile her. "Eden has a point."

"Very well," Ralston agreed with exasperation at their disorganization. "Falcone, please explain the intel you learned this morning. I filled everyone in about your sighting of Lady

Langdale but have not had a chance yet to tell them everything else."

Falcone rose and stood with his hands behind his back. "While on surveillance of Lady Langdale's home, I saw a carriage waiting outside the residence. I couldn't get close enough to recognize the coat of arms, but the lady who exited Lady Langdale's home appeared well-to-do."

"What did she look like?" Worth questioned.

"She was an older lady and quite stunning. Her hair is the color of soft butter with streaks of sunshine. The style of her clothing is of the latest trends. My guess is that she helps Lady Langdale with the seduction of her victims," Falcone explained.

"What brought you to that assumption?" Kincaid asked.

"Because, Lord Kincaid, I followed the carriage. It traveled into the shadier part of London to collect Lady L's goons, then picked up some poor bloke. The carriage then proceeded out of town."

"Did you continue to follow them?" Kincaid drilled Falcone.

"No."

Kincaid threw his hands in the air. "Why ever not? We need solid proof of Lady L's arrival in London. Not hearsay."

"They were her men," Falcone snarled.

"Then you should have stayed close to confirm her sighting. Instead, you let her get away," Kincaid accused.

Kincaid and Falcone had advanced on the other while making their arguments.

Ralston stepped between them, holding his arms out to keep them apart. "Arguing with each other will not help our case."

"The work of an amateur," Kincaid muttered. "Where is Dracott? He would never have made such a foolish mistake."

"Who is this Dracott?" Falcone asked. "Can we trust him?"

"I hired him a few months ago," Worth stated.

"Why?" Falcone asked.

Worth defended his actions. "Because we needed more help. You were unavailable."

"Because I was tracking Lady L on the Continent," Falcone snarled. "Not playing cards at balls or chasing skirts around town."

"We each had our own part to play. You are the one who made the choice to leave the country," Worth argued.

Falcone glared at Worth. "I had my reasons. You never answered my question. Can we trust Dracott? How do we know he is not a spy for Lady Langdale?"

Eden gasped. "Because he is an honorable gentleman."

Falcone quirked an eyebrow at her. "Unlike myself?"

"Yes," Eden hissed.

"Enough!" Ralston declared. "Trading insults between one another solves nothing. Everyone take a seat so we can discuss this rationally."

Before they sat down, Reese stalked into the office, waving around a letter. "Where is he?"

"Who?" Worth asked.

"Dracott," Reese snarled.

Eden and Worth exchanged worried looks. Reese had worked himself into a snit, and it didn't bode well for Dracott. Was Reese the reason for Dracott's disappearance? If so, what had he done? The only reason for Reese's anger was because Dracott had hurt Maggie.

"He is following a lead on one of our cases," Worth explained.

"Is this the same case you have kept a secret from me? One that involves my ex-mistress," Reese demanded.

Nobody answered Reese. They each wore a guilty expression from keeping their investigation under wraps. In their defense, they did so to protect Reese and Evelyn from Lady L's evilness. They were targets who needed protection.

"In all fairness, our investigation is a business matter," Ralston explained.

Reese shook his head in disgust. "Business matter." He scoffed. "This far surpasses business. She has made it a personal matter."

Reese threw the letter at Worth. The longer Worth read the letter, the more shocked his expression turned. He passed it to Eden next, and she scoured the missive. The accusations the letter held far surpassed a shocking reaction. It painted a story of deception and greed. She looked up in horror at her brothers.

"No," Eden denied, shaking her head.

Barbara Langdale's letter told the story of two brothers who set out to destroy the Worthington family under her direction. She took great pleasure in giving details of her plan to make Reese suffer for abandoning her all those years ago. Her vindictiveness led her to break the hearts of his sisters. Since she couldn't hurt him, she would torment those he loved.

"I am afraid so. Colebourne confirmed the story of Ravencroft's family history," Reese stated.

"Maggie? Noel?" Eden only spoke their names. No other question needed to be asked.

"They don't know yet. I will deal with Dracott in my own way," Reese threatened.

"You cannot," Worth said.

"I can and I will," Reese bit out. "He is a nobody, and no one will miss him."

Worth tried to get his brother to see reason. "Ravencroft will notice."

Eden gripped the letter in her hand. "So you will destroy Dracott because he is not a peer. But Ravencroft will not suffer because of his standing in society."

"Oh, Ravencroft will suffer, but he will do so under my watch," Reese growled.

"It is unfair." Eden slammed her hand down on the desk.

"Unfair?" Reese roared. "These gentlemen have ruined our sisters. They do not deserve fair."

Ralston, always the peacemaker, stepped forward and guided Eden to sit down. After he took the letter from her hand and read it, he shook his head and passed it over to Kincaid. Once Kincaid read it, he folded it and placed it in his pocket.

"What? Do I not deserve to understand what is transpiring?" Falcone asked.

"No," Kincaid stated and turned to Reese. "What do you need from us?"

"I want both gentlemen found and I will deliver their punishment." Reese spoke in a deadly, harsh whisper.

"Falcone, please see my sister home," Worth ordered.

"No!" Eden shouted.

"Falcone. Now!" Worth demanded.

Falcone snarled his displeasure at how they dismissed him so easily. However, he never uttered a word. He stalked over to Eden and waited for her to rise. She glared at her brothers, but when they wouldn't relent, she rose with dignity and stormed out of the office. He followed her outside. She stood on the walkway, tapping her foot with annoyance. While he didn't appreciate his colleagues treating him like a lap dog, hc would learn what the letter held.

Eden Worthington was a fine lady. Polished and always displayed impeccable manners. However, when the lady's temper rose, she acted before thinking. He only needed to fuel her fury, and soon she would spill everything he needed to know.

"Hurry, Falcone. I do not have all day. I must return home at once."

Falcone gritted his teeth at her snide tone. Oh, how he wanted to set her in her place. Perhaps even make her think twice before treating him as she did. One day he would. Only not today. But one day soon, he would find pleasure in her downfall from grace.

Falcone opened the door to his carriage. "Your chariot awaits, my lady."

Eden glared at him. She settled on the seat and waited for Falcone to give instructions to the driver. Once he sat across from her and the carriage set off, his smirk returned. She knew what he expected, and she refused to allow her fury at her brothers to play into his hands. Her brothers, Ralston, and Kincaid kept the details of the letter to themselves for a reason. They didn't trust Falcone, and she didn't either. It wasn't because he gave them any excuse not to trust him. However, it was a family matter and would stay in the family. Ralston and Kincaid were an extended branch of their family and would keep the secret amongst themselves.

She wouldn't betray her sisters' heartache for anything. Eden worried about how they would react. She understood Reese's meaning about how he would handle the gentlemen. She only hoped Graham talked sense into him concerning Dracott. It would break Maggie's heart if anything happened to him. She had watched her sister fall head over heels in love with Dracott. He was Maggie's soulmate. Noel wouldn't suffer because Reese would still allow her to wed Ravencroft, since he held a title. She would learn nothing different.

Eden's thoughts consumed her, and she soon forgot about Falcone across from her. The gentlemen must have an explanation for their deceit. She had gotten to know Dracott quite well and didn't believe he had played Maggie false. But then she had to wonder if the letter held any truth. After all, Ravencroft and Dracott had fooled their entire family into believing they had never met before, when in fact they were brothers.

The carriage pulled up to her townhome, and Falcone stepped down to help her out. She flew up the walk with Falcone following her. She must stop him before he entered the house.

Eden turned around and placed her hand on his chest. "You are no longer needed, Lord Falcone."

"So it is your family's intention to keep me in the dark," Falcone snarled.

Eden smiled for the first time since she read the letter, taking immense pleasure in his unhappiness. "Yes."

Falcone growled. "I insist on knowing what the letter stated."

She shook her head. "Sorry. I seemed to have forgotten what it said."

"Like hell you did."

"Tsk, tsk. Such language. 'Tis most improper of you to speak in that manner in front of a lady," Eden baited him.

"Lady? 'Tis questionable," Falcone returned in full.

Eden laughed. "Good day, Lord Falcone."

She swept inside and slammed the door in his face. Any other time, she would have gloated in besting Lord Falcone. But she must find Maggie. Perhaps her sister had knowledge of Dracott's identity. If not, then Eden must deliver the dreadful news.

The chaos had exploded into a colossal mess.

Eden hurried along the hallway, searching for Maggie in every room. She couldn't afford to run into their mother.

Mama would notice her distress and demand to learn what troubled her. She must find her sister before Reese and Graham returned home. She needed to tell Maggie about Lady Langdale's letter and see if Maggie held knowledge about the secrets Dracott kept. Reese and Graham would return home after they discussed a plan with Ralston and Kincaid to search for Ravencroft and Dracott. Reese's demands would provoke Maggie to act out with irrational behavior.

"Lady Eden, you are home sooner than I expected." Rogers startled Eden in her search.

Eden clutched her chest, calming herself. "Yes. I must speak with Maggie. Have you seen her?"

"She is in the nursery, playing with Lady Mina," Rogers answered.

"All right." Eden's gaze drifted to the door, expecting her brothers to storm through. "Please send the nanny to the nursery."

Rogers noted Lady Eden's distress and wished to help her. "Is there a matter I may offer my assistance with?"

Eden took a deep breath. She must gather her emotions under control. If not, Rogers would inform her mother. She gave Rogers a serene smile. "Thank you, but no. I am excited to share some news with Maggie."

Rogers gave her a skeptical stare. "Very well. I shall send the nanny at once."

Eden nodded. "Excellent."

She hurried off, climbing the stairs in a rush. Eden found Maggie playing teatime with Mina. She glanced behind her with impatience. She had hoped to go unnoticed until the nanny arrived, but Maggie saw her.

"Look who has joined us for tea." Maggie pointed at Eden.

Mina squealed with glee. "Aunt Eden, hurry before Lady Hogabiscuit takes your seat."

Eden smiled at her niece with adoration. If she wasn't desperate to talk with Maggie, she would've played with them. However, today she must disappoint Mina.

"I am sorry, poppet. But Maggie and I are late, and we must hurry," Eden explained. "I promise to play with you tomorrow."

Maggie looked confused, and Eden gave her a small shake of her head not to ask questions. The nanny rushed into the nursery.

"All right," Mina said, already pouring tea for the nanny.

Eden nodded for Maggie to follow her. After Maggie kissed Mina goodbye, Eden rushed Maggie along to her bedchamber.

"We have little time," Eden started.

"For what?" Maggie gave Eden a peculiar stare.

Eden's desperate attempt to get her alone confused Maggie. Was Eden in trouble? Eden still hadn't answered her question. Instead, she paced back and forth across Maggie's bedchamber, nibbling on her fingernails in between muttering about temperamental brothers and gentlemen who played her sisters false.

Maggie tensed at the comments. Eden wasn't in trouble. This was all about Crispin. What had she learned? And what did Reese and Graham know? Her sister wouldn't behave in this manner if her brothers hadn't learned about Crispin's secrets.

"Tell me what you have learned," Maggie demanded.

Eden paused and faced her sister. "Are you aware Dracott is Ravencroft's half-brother?"

Maggie nodded. "I learned last night of their connection."

Eden's eyebrows drew together. "How? You have not seen Dracott for days."

"I snuck out and visited him at his lodgings," Maggie confessed.

Eden gasped before her face fell. "Oh, Mags. What have you done?"

The implications of Maggie's visit to Dracott's was clear by her sister's expression. The blush spreading along her neck only added to the evidence of how they had spent her visit. Reese's plan to make Dracott disappear wasn't an option any longer. There could be consequences to their evening spent together. Dracott had ruined Maggie for any other suitors. Which left Eden to wonder if the situation could escalate further out of control.

However, before Eden learned what else Maggie knew, Reese's thunderous roar called for Maggie. Instead of cowering, her sister stood up straight and threw her shoulders back, marching to the door.

"Wait, Maggie. 'Tis not as simple as Reese being unhappy with Dracott's courtship. Something more sinister is at play. Reese is furious and will make demands you will want to defy. Let me speak with him first. Evelyn, Mama, and I will make him see reason," Eden warned.

Maggie turned, offering Eden a courageous smile. "No. 'Tis my burden to defend. I may not know Crispin's story to explain to Reese. But I hold faith in our love for one another."

Reese threw the bedchamber's door open and stormed inside, followed by Graham and Evelyn. "Downstairs in my study, now!" Reese pointed for Maggie to obey his orders.

Maggie nodded, and with her head held high, she started for the stairs.

"Reese, what is this about?" Evelyn tugged on his arm.

Evelyn's softly spoken question transformed Reese into a caring husband. His gaze softened as he looked at his wife. He didn't wish to worry her, but the threats Barbara Langdale made in her letter would affect their family greatly. While he couldn't hide the facts from her, he could protect her to the best of his abilities. He must calm down before causing her any stress.

"Sometimes, my love, other people fool us with their false impressions. And it is my duty to deal with the deception." Reese squeezed Evelyn's hand before following Maggie.

"Who was false?" Evelyn asked.

"Dracott," Eden whispered.

"And Ravencroft," Graham snarled. "Where is Noel?"

"She and Mama went shopping. I felt ill, so I stayed at home," Evelyn answered.

Graham nodded before leaving.

Evelyn walked over to Eden and grabbed her hands. "What have you learned?"

"They are brothers. You must stop Reese. He means to destroy Dracott and he cannot. Maggie and Dracott have shared intimate relations," Eden explained.

"Oh my. Is the matter that severe?"

"Yes. I am afraid so."

"Then we must join them." Evelyn tugged Eden after her.

Evelyn and Eden rushed along the hallway. Someone pounded at the front door, and Reese ordered Rogers to get rid of any unwanted visitors.

"Only allow Ralston and Kincaid entry. However, if Ravencroft or Dracott are bold enough to call, then by all means, show them to my study and bring along my pistols," Reese commanded.

The ladies paused on the staircase at Reese's harsh instructions. His fury had returned, and if Evelyn didn't stay by his side throughout this ordeal, she feared for the bloodshed that would spill.

Rogers waited to open the door until after Reese entered his study. Evelyn expected to make excuses to a friend, not for the sight that greeted them. Dracott stumbled inside with his face covered in blood, clutching at his side.

"Maggie," he croaked between his lips before he fell at Rogers's feet.

Rogers glanced along the hallway, then at Evelyn before taking action. He heaved Dracott to his feet. "Help me," he ordered the footman.

The ladies followed Rogers as he carried Dracott to his quarters. He asked the footman to gather a list of supplies. After the servant rushed away, the butler started cleaning Dracott's wounds.

"Rogers?" Evelyn questioned.

Rogers lowered his head before meeting her gaze with a wounded expression. "Forgive me, my lady, for disobeying your husband's orders. You may dismiss me for my refusal to obey. However, the boy needs care, and I made a promise that I must fulfill."

Evelyn held no clue about what transpired before them. But Rogers's feelings for Dracott were clear. He cared for the man and held regret for not protecting him. Secret upon secret kept coming forth. And she knew from experience that if the truth stayed hidden, it would destroy many lives.

Evelyn placed her hand on Rogers's shoulder in comfort. "You take care of Lord Dracott, and I will handle Lord Worthington. Do not worry."

"Thank you, my lady." He continued making Dracott more comfortable.

Evelyn motioned for Eden to follow her. "Stay near and offer Rogers your help. I will see to Reese. If Rogers or Dracott tries to leave, come tell us immediately. For Maggie's sake, we must keep Dracott here."

"I agree. Hurry, before he scares Maggie off to search for Dracott. We also learned earlier how Maggie has become a target. Her life is in danger," Eden explained.

"By whom?"

Eden winced. "Lady Langdale."

Evelyn gritted her teeth. "Like hell. She will not harm any member of my family."

Evelyn hurried to Reese's study and found that Mama and Noel had returned home. Mama shot her a distressed look, and Evelyn shrugged at how she was unclear about the situation. She was still at a loss about what had infuriated her husband.

"Why is Ravencroft forbidden from entering our home?" Noel whined.

Reese crossed his arms in front of his chest. "Because I have decided on what is best for our family."

Noel cried out. "This is unfair."

"One day you will understand." He moved to sit behind his desk. His action displayed his declaration as final.

"Mama?" Noel pleaded.

Mama hugged Noel. "I am sorry, my dear. I cannot argue your case against your brother until he informs us why he has made this decision. Calm down while we listen to his explanation."

Reese folded his hands on top of the desk. His mother thought it was a simple misunderstanding that provoked him to make his demands. He looked around the room at his family, and remorse settled over him. They would all fall victim to the mistakes of his past. It was time to explain the letter he had received and how he would handle matters. He noticed Eden had not joined them.

"Where is Eden?" Reese asked Evelyn.

Evelyn sat down in a chair near his desk. "She is helping Rogers with a slight issue."

"What issue?"

Evelyn folded her hands in her lap. "A guest arrived, and she is helping the person settle."

"What guest? I gave Rogers an order," Reese growled.

"We can discuss the guest later. Please tell us why you behave like the world has ended." Evelyn gave her husband a look to continue.

Reese sighed, not wishing to argue with his wife. "Very well."

"I do not care what Reese says. I am of age and no longer require his permission," Noel declared before running from the study.

Mama cried after her. "Noel?"

"Let her go, Mama. Give her a moment to herself and allow Reese to explain," Graham urged.

Mama pointed her finger at Reese. "Stop your stalling and proceed. We are all grown adults and do not need coddled. You cannot allow these gentlemen to court your sisters and then withdraw your consent without an explanation."

"I very well can. And you will agree with my decision once you hear why," Reese stated smugly.

"Heaven forbid a man's arrogance," Mama muttered.

Evelyn chuckled. She couldn't help herself. Her mother-in-law's comment helped to ease the tension. Graham joined in with her laughter, and Reese smirked. However, Maggie's plea reminded them of the severity of their dilemma.

"Please tell us the reason for your anger," Maggie requested quietly.

Chapter Seventeen

T HE COOL TOUCH OF a rag on his wounds awakened Dracott from his misery. He peeled open one eye and found Eden Worthington wiping blood off his knuckles. His other eye had swollen shut. Rogers sat on his other side, cleaning his face. He groaned over the beating his body had taken. The brutes had enjoyed trouncing him, making it the worst he had ever received. He tried pulling himself up.

"Lie still, Lord Dracott, before you do yourself any more harm," Eden ordered.

"I must explain to Maggie," Dracott scraped out.

Eden sighed. "It has reached beyond confessing your sins to Maggie. You must confess them to our entire family. Reese is out for your blood because of your deception."

Dracott brushed their hands away. He would survive. He always did. "Take me to them."

He swung his legs over the bed. However, before he rose, a rush of dizziness swept over him, crippling his strength.

Rogers's arms pulled him back and forced him to lie down. "You are in no shape," Rogers growled.

He opened his eye and stared at him. "I have dealt with worse. Do not blame yourself."

Rogers shook his head. "I promised your father, and I failed."

"No," Dracott denied. "This is no one's fault but my own. My actions caught up with me."

"I will make her pay," Rogers swore.

Dracott grasped his hand. "No, you will stay away from her. Promise me. I cannot stand to lose you, too."

Rogers clutched at Dracott's hand, fighting his need to seek revenge. He would promise the boy for now while he recovered. Then he would strike with his vengeance at Lady Langdale and Lady Ravencroft. Both ladies would rue the day they messed with his family. He nodded his head in agreement, too choked to speak.

Eden watched the exchange, curious now more than ever to learn about their connection. Dracott's beating gave proof of his allegiance to them. Lady L wouldn't have sought this punishment for someone she relied on. What had Dracott done to bring the lady's wrath upon him? A beating to this extent showed Lady L sought her revenge for Dracott's betrayal.

Eden poured Dracott a cup of tea filled with healing herbs. "Drink this. It will help your throat." Dracott did her bidding, watching her with a weariness Eden herself felt. "I only have one question for you."

Dracott nodded for her to ask about it.

"Do you love Maggie?"

"With all my heart and soul. I will move heaven and hell to protect her. You have my promise," Dracott answered.

Eden sat back in the chair. "Very well. Finish your tea, and we shall join my family." She looked over at the butler. "And you too, Rogers. You have your own share of secrets to confess."

Rogers nodded in agreement.

After Dracott finished his tea, Eden stepped out of the room for Dracott to dress into a fresh change of clothing. She had sent a servant to collect them from Graham's bedchamber.

She didn't want the sight of bloodied clothes to scare Maggie. Dracott's face would be painful enough for her sister to see.

With Rogers on Dracott's one side and a footman on his other, Eden led them to Reese's study. "Are you ready? This will not be a pleasant exchange."

"No, it will not. But one I will attempt with what honor I have. I am ready to unburden my secrets. They've been a heavy load to carry," Dracott confessed.

Eden dismissed the servant and offered her arm to Dracott. He attempted a smile at her support, but his lips ached from the simple act.

"Thank you," he whispered.

"Break her heart and I will not be so kind," Eden threatened before opening the door.

Rogers and Eden helped Dracott inside. Reese stormed around his desk and advanced on them with his arm pulled back. Graham noticed Dracott's face and Eden's support and stepped in front of Reese, blocking him from doing Dracott any more harm. Mama gasped.

Maggie rushed forward. "Crispin," she cried.

Maggie stood in front of Crispin in shock. Her hand trembled as she brushed her fingers across the bruise on his cheek. He flinched but didn't pull away. His sigh at her touch broke her heart in two.

"What happened?" Maggie whispered.

"You have some nerve showing your face," Reese growled.

"I am sorry, love. I wanted to share this in private." Crispin covered his hand over Maggie's.

"You have lost that chance," Reese snarled.

"I am sure he is aware of the circumstances before him," Graham replied sarcastically. "Why don't we let Dracott sit down." He guided Maggie away.

Eden and Rogers settled Dracott on the sofa, and Maggie moved to his side. Eden sat down on the other side of Maggie and grabbed her hand, showing her support.

"That will be all, Rogers. Thank you for your help," Lady Worthington said.

"No, Mama. Rogers has his own secrets to confess." Eden pointed at the chair closest to Dracott, and Rogers nodded.

After everyone returned to their seats, the room grew quiet. Maggie slid her other hand into Crispin's, and tears slid along her cheeks as she stared at his beaten features. She squeezed his hand, and he brought it to his lips, kissing her fingers. Reese growled his dislike, but Dracott refused to take the hint. His need to reassure Maggie mattered more to him.

"You have exactly five seconds to drop my sister's hand or else I will find pleasure in finishing your beating," Reese threatened.

Everyone but Dracott and Rogers reprimanded Reese. Still, Dracott defied him and held on.

Reese started to countdown. "Five. Four."

Graham interrupted. "Dracott, we received some disturbing news from a source today, stating you were Lord Ravencroft's half-brother. Is this information correct?"

Dracott cleared his throat. "Lady Langdale, I presume."

Graham nodded.

"Yes. The information is correct," Dracott confirmed.

"The letter also states of your involvement with the thievery ring you help to investigate. Also, it explains your role in planting decoys to stall our progress and how your key role is to seduce my sister," Graham continued.

"Lies." Dracott kept his gaze focused on Graham.

Reese scoffed. "Do you expect us to believe you?"

Dracott shifted his gaze toward Reese. "No, my lord. I do not expect you to."

Reese tightened his hands on the arm of the chair. "What do you have to say for yourself?"

"I have no knowledge about what I am to defend myself over. May I read the letter?" Dracott held his hand out.

Graham looked at Reese, and his brother nodded his approval. He handed the letter over to Dracott. Maggie caught Graham's gaze and implored him in a silent message to hear Dracott out. Hell, didn't she understand how he didn't want to think the worse of Dracott. He considered the man his friend and had trusted him with his life. But the evidence was damning. However, he gave her a small smile to show he would.

Maggie breathed a sigh of relief at Graham's offer of support. Oh, she knew he only smiled to pacify her. However, Graham always stood in her corner, and she held faith that he would remain so with this matter. She focused on Crispin again and watched his features change dramatically. His gaze hardened the more he read, and he crumpled the letter and threw it on the floor after he finished reading it.

What did the letter state? She bent over to retrieve the letter, but Crispin stopped her. He shook his head. She wanted to read the details of the letter. Yet her heart cried out at the lies it held, and she wanted no part of it. Whoever this Lady Langdale was, she meant to destroy them, and Maggie chose not to give her the power. She sat back against the cushions.

"Well?" Reese asked.

"If you will remain patient with me, I want to share with you my past, my present, and my future. I will not go into the details about my past, but I will give you enough information to help you understand my motives. My only request is that you will wait until I am finished before asking your questions," Dracott started.

Dracott looked at Rogers before he continued, and Rogers nodded his approval. "My correct name is Crispin Dracott Rogers. I am the bastard child of Mr. Clyde Rogers and Lady Ravencroft. I hold no title, nor will I ever. Rogers is my uncle, my father's brother. After my father passed away, my mother found herself involved with Lady Langdale. I spent my formable years as a lackey with the pack of thieves, doing whatever Lady L demanded to survive. Rogers tried many times to intervene without luck. After I refused to abandon my mother, Rogers left in frustration. A couple of years later, to my surprise, I learned I had a brother."

He paused and drew in a breath. His mouth ached to talk, but he had only just started. "In his search to find his mother, Ravencroft discovered he also had a brother. When he realized the debt our mother owed, he refused to leave. He stayed until we cleared the debt. Then he secured us passage to return to his estate. However, we learned you can never leave Lady L's clutches if you wish to live."

Dracott glanced around the room, noting everyone's expressions. They were eager to ask him questions, but they waited patiently for him to finish.

"We were only on the estate for a short time before she made her demands to join her thievery ring again or for us to meet our demise. She gave us a deadline. Ravencroft thought if he came to London alone, he could find allies to help him defeat her. When he never sent word and the deadline drew near, I panicked and left the estate, following him here. Only once I reached London did I realize I couldn't claim Ravencroft as my brother. It would draw forth too many questions. So I altered my name, changed my appearance, and attempted my own search to bring about Lady L's demise."

He looked at Graham. "I heard about your outfit and the rest you know after that. I want to destroy her, and I have faith we can. That is my past and now onto my present. Lady L made threats against your family once she learned of our connection."

Reese interrupted. "Maggie and Noel."

"Yes. She threatened to expose Ravencroft to the ton for his past involvement with her crew. She wanted him to steal the blueprints to your townhome because she plans a heist during Maggie's debutante ball. Her plan is to seek her revenge on you for throwing her over. She will stop at nothing until she destroys your family. If Ravencroft didn't supply her with the prints by her deadline, she threatened to kidnap Maggie."

"Why Maggie and not Noel?" Graham asked.

Dracott grimaced. "Because she learned of my arrival and how I paid court on Maggie. Lady Langdale knows how Ravencroft would go to any lengths to protect my happiness. She learned how he regretted my troubled life while he spent his time in an indulgent lifestyle. She played on him to help her. When he never secured her wish, she brought our mother to town to help her cause."

"I thought your mother was dead," Eden stated.

Dracott shook his head. "Unfortunately not. However, I can understand why you would assume so. Ravencroft must have implied his mother was no longer in his life, hoping that you would presume he meant she had died. No. She lives, and she gave him an ultimatum to introduce her to your family or become victims to Lady Langdale. Since he missed the deadline, Lady L has started her terror. The destruction began with her letter and my beating."

"Where is Lord Ravencroft?" Evelyn asked.

"That I do not know. I can only assume he has holed himself up in his townhome, drinking his sorrows away. He knows he failed and what is about to begin. He is drinking his courage to face your family. I pleaded with him weeks ago, but he wanted to figure out a plan on his own, even when he realized how hopeless it was. But he has his pride."

"And your future?" Lady Worthington asked.

Dracott looked over at Maggie and smiled. She never once released his hand while he admitted to his deceit. The soft smile she granted him gave him the encouragement he needed to answer her mother's question. She was his world, and he loved her with all his heart. The love shining from her eyes calmed his soul like it always did.

He took a deep breath. "With your permission, I wish to marry Maggie. I may not have much to offer her but the stability of my love. I will work hard with your family to destroy Lady L and show Maggie how much I love her every day. If you refuse, then I shall return to seek your permission until you say yes. Because I need her more than I need the air to breathe. I could spout a list of why I love her and how she is the other half of my soul. However, you only need to understand I will love her for eternity and protect her with my heart."

"No!" Reese's denial struck Dracott like lightning. The force of one simple word held an impact he couldn't explain. Yet it gave him hope at the same time.

"That is not your decision to make," Lady Worthington informed Reese.

"Mother," Reese warned.

She smiled patiently at her eldest child. "I am her parent. While I've allowed you to handle certain aspects over the years to ease my burden, this is a decision I will make."

"But he lied to our family," Reese argued.

"Out of love. You of all people should understand more than anyone else," Mama explained.

Her comment quieted Reese. Maggie's mother turned her attention to Dracott. She didn't speak for a while and merely gazed at him. Eventually, she nodded once she made her decision.

"I sympathize with you, Crispin. My heart breaks for the pain you have endured in your trials of life. I know of your mother. You see, she ran with the same pack of degenerates as my husband did. As a mother, I weep at the horror of your scars, and I only wish to wrap you in my arms to soothe them away. While you will always suffer from those memories, I hope with the love of my daughter they will fade away. You have my permission and the support of our family." She focused her gaze on Maggie. "However, I am not the one to ask."

Lady Worthington's words astounded Dracott. He stood up and walked to her. "You have humbled me."

Lady Worthington rose and wrapped him in a hug. "No, my son. I am the one who is humbled. I shall warn you, though, this hug is the first of many." She winked at him. "That is, if she answers yes."

Her light tease prompted Dracott into action. He limped over to Maggie and held out his hand. She placed her palm next to his, and he fought back the tears wanting to fall. His confession and the love he held for the lady before him strung out his emotions.

He linked their fingers together. "My love. I have spent a lifetime wishing for an angel to save me from my hell. When I watched you ride across your land the first day we met, I knew I had found her. You have reawakened my soul with every moment we've spent together. I love you and will spend a lifetime showing you if you would do me the honor of becoming my bride. Will you marry me?"

"Yes," Maggie choked out.

Tears fell like raindrops on their hands. She cried for both of them. She had no poetic lines of love to deliver to him. His words turned her into a bumbling mess.

"Yes. Yes. Yes." Maggie was incapable of uttering any other words. Later, she would express her love to him, away from her family.

"Well, she did play with Mina today," Eden teased.

Everyone erupted into laughter because Maggie sounded like Mina whenever she chanted something.

Crispin leaned over and brushed his lips against Maggie's in a chaste kiss. When she gave him a secretive smile, he chuckled. The minx would keep their life exciting and never dull. Soon, Maggie's family pulled her into their hugs. Rogers placed his hand on his shoulder in a gesture of affection. He never spoke during their meeting, but they knew the Worthington gentlemen would address him once the ladies left the study.

Graham shook his hand. "Welcome to the family. Do not worry, Reese will come around."

Dracott nodded. However, he was unsure if the earl would ever forgive him. Only time would tell. He was the only one who didn't offer his congratulations. But it didn't seem to bother Maggie any. She laughed with her sister and Evelyn while her mother watched on.

"Crispin, you will stay with us while you recover and until the wedding. After you and Maggie wed, you may decide if you wish to stay or rent a place of your own. Rogers will send a footman to collect your belongings. Maggie, why do we not leave the gentlemen to finish their business? You can help Evelyn choose a bedchamber for your groom."

Lady Worthington never gave him a chance to refuse her offer. She swept out of the study, calling for the ladies to follow her. Maggie blew him a kiss over her shoulder, happy to accommodate her mother's request. Evelyn spoke a few quiet words to her husband, while Eden spoke to Graham.

After the ladies left, Worthington moved behind his desk to display his authority. Worth moved to stand next to him, and Worthington pointed at the chairs in front of the desk for them to sit.

"I will make this quick, Dracott. I will respect my mother's and sister's wishes. However, until I see you are no longer a threat to this family, I will keep my eye on you. You will remain under this roof until that day. Are we in agreement?" Worthington demanded.

Dracott sat up straight in his seat and met Worthington's stare. "Yes. I understand how I need to earn your trust. Also, it is best for Maggie to remain under your protection until we catch Lady Langdale. That goes for every lady in this household. You will need Kincaid's men for protection. My advice is not to alarm the ladies until it is necessary. However, you must make them understand there is an element of danger lurking at your door."

"Sound advice, Dracott," Worth said.

Worthington steepled his fingers together. "We will finish this discussion tomorrow once Ralston and Kincaid are present. However, for now, I will address your involvement, Rogers. How did you end up as my butler? It is no coincidence."

Rogers nodded. "No, it is not. But you must seek your explanation elsewhere. When this day came forth, I was to inform you of the gentleman's name you must speak with for your answers."

Worthington arched an eyebrow. "And who might that be?"

Rogers winced. "Colebourne."

Rogers was met with a deadly stare. Dracott shifted in his seat in fear for his uncle's safety at the fury in Worthington's eyes. However, Rogers's answer only seemed to amuse Worth.

"Not you too?" Worth chuckled.

"I am afraid so, sir," Rogers answered.

"I am confused," Dracott stated.

"My wife's uncle has acquired an assortment of people who owe him debts. And he collects those debts by making them perform his biddings," Worthington explained.

Dracott didn't understand how Rogers's employment in Worthington's household, attained years ago, played a part in the dilemma before them now. But he had a hunch he would learn how far Colebourne intertwined himself in their investigation after he married Maggie.

"You may go, Rogers. I am finished with you," Worthington ordered.

"Are you dismissing me?" Rogers asked.

"No. Colebourne placed you here for a reason, and until you no longer suit his purpose, you will remain. However, my sentiments toward Dracott are the same for you."

Rogers bowed. "Understandable, my lord. Thank you."

Once Rogers left, Worthington pointed to the bottle of whiskey and glasses. "Make yourself useful," he told Worth.

Worth chuckled, pouring each gentleman a glass. Both brothers kicked their drink back in one shot, while Dracott sipped at his. The spirit stung his torn lip.

"To patience," Worth toasted.

"Hell! Do you not mean to make a toast to his sanity?" Worthington asked.

Throughout the afternoon, Maggie's brothers made more toasts, teasing him about his union with Maggie. It was during those toasts he realized how Worthington understood his actions, but his first priority was to protect his sister. Dracott respected Worthington for that alone. While the brothers continued to torment him, he also realized what it felt like to be part of a family. He hoped his brother realized this too and would come around.

If not, then he would take it upon himself to make sure he did.

Chapter Eighteen

D RACOTT SIGHED AS HE sank into the mattress. His tortured
body moaned at the pleasure of comfort. He didn't know
how to express his gratitude to this family, except to make
good on his promise to love Maggie for a lifetime. A promise
he would fulfill with pleasure.

A soft hand slid along his arm, and whisper-soft kisses
caressed his sores. He hadn't realized he had fallen asleep. He
opened his eyes to find Maggie at his side.

"Maggie," he whispered.

She placed a finger on his lips. "Shh. Let me speak. You
spoke so eloquently in front of my family of the love you hold
for me. Your words left me speechless. I want to express the
feelings I hold for you."

"There is no need, my love. I can feel them here," Crispin
reassured her, drawing her hand over his heart.

"I want to." She took a deep breath. "I am nowhere near the
poet you are, my love. However, I can express how your love
makes me feel like I am floating on air, and I know you will
catch me when I fall. The first time I saw you, you awakened
my soul. You understood me without even knowing me. I want
us to spend a lifetime learning everything about each other. I
understand the secrets you keep are painful or perhaps even

shameful to share with me. But I hope in time you will because I will keep your secrets guarded close to my heart. And if you choose not to, it will never alter my love any. The only secret I hold is how I prefer to dress like a boy and ride horses. Also, I detest wearing dresses and acting like a lady. But my friends and family have knowledge of that secret."

Crispin pulled Maggie to him and kissed her with all the love in his heart. It was the first kiss of many they would share. When Maggie moaned, he fought with himself to pull away.

"I am sorry, my love. While I wish nothing more than to strip this robe from your body and worship you with sweet kisses, I will not disrespect your family. We will wait until our wedding night before we make love again. I should never have been so selfish before and taken your virtue. I should have waited like a proper gentleman."

Maggie's laughter teased his senses. "'Twas not a gentleman I wanted."

He rolled Maggie over and hovered above her. "Is that so? What did you want?"

She brushed the hair from his forehead. "I wanted the man whose eyes spoke of danger, whose touch set my soul on fire, and whose kisses stole my very breath away. The very man who just asked me to become his bride today."

"Ah, Mags, you undo me."

He couldn't help himself. He needed to taste her lips again. Maggie wrapped her arms around his neck, urging his mouth to hers. However, he needed no encouragement. He ravished her lips like a starving man. These past few days without her had been torture enough. While he suffered through his beating, his mind had only thought of his salvation. Maggie. Crispin fed his soul with one kiss after another. He never let his hands stray and kept them still, holding her in his embrace. He meant what he said, and he promised himself to honor it.

Once her kisses satisfied him, Crispin settled her in his arms. They lay there for a while in silence, content to be together. However, Maggie couldn't stay still and rolled over, propping herself on his chest. She would never tire of staring at him.

"Maggie?"

"Mmm." She placed a kiss on his chest.

"I want to share my secrets with you."

"You do not have to."

This time, he placed his finger against her lips. "I want to. I will not go in depth about them tonight. However, I want to tell you a little of my past. And of another secret that I must ask you to keep from your family."

She curved her hands against his cheeks. "I promise you I will guard your secrets as my own."

Crispin took a deep breath. He wasn't proud of what he was about to confess, but he didn't want any secrets between them. If he wanted to become a better man, then he must overcome his past.

"I was a young boy when my mother became involved with Lady Langdale. However, they thought I was old enough to partake in their schemes. They used me as a decoy to distract their intended target. Sometimes I had to pretend I had become separated from my parents, and other times I had to steal something small to have them chase after me. While I caused a distraction, they would sneak in and steal from their marks. Then, while they were deep into their cups celebrating their heists, they would use me for entertainment."

Maggie frowned. "How?"

He avoided her eyes. "As a punching bag. They would place bets on who would knock me down. After about the third time, I realized the games they played. So I fell to the ground after the first punch. Well, this only infuriated them, and they found other ways to torture me. None of them were pleasant.

However, once Ravencroft arrived, he put a stop to it. But the damage had already been set."

"Was the terror you suffered through the other night a result of their torment?" Maggie asked.

"Yes. I had a flashback, and it triggered an episode. I am so sorry, Maggie, for scaring you." His voice hitched.

"Shh. There are no apologies in healing, my love."

"I do not deserve you, but I refuse to let you go."

Maggie smiled. "Good."

His hand trembled as he ran it through her curls. "Once I grew older and matured, Lady L used me for different purposes. My role changed, or should I say the way I attempted to distract the mark changed."

"How so?"

Crispin sighed with the shame he must admit to. "My job was to seduce the ladies by any means possible."

"Oh." Maggie's brows drew together in confusion and then widened. "Oh!" Her gaze dropped from his. "Oh."

"I am not proud of my actions, nor can I explain why I stayed. Other than I had no clue any other life was possible. Also, my mother had secured our fate each time she borrowed money and never paid Lady L back."

Maggie listened to Crispin's explanation. She raised her head and met his eyes. She saw his suffering and shame and wanted to soothe him. But she couldn't. He must do so on his own. No matter how much his time with other women bothered her, it was before she met him. She wouldn't condemn him for his past actions. His behavior from this day forth was all that mattered.

"I am sorry for the life your mother forced you to live. Sometimes it is the actions of our past that shape the person we are today. And you, Crispin Dracott, show proof of someone who has overcome the ghosts of his past."

"Not completely, but I will continue to fight them for you," Crispin swore.

"And the secret you wish for me to keep?" Maggie asked.

"Graham has asked me to search for a lady. She is a friend of mine from my past, and I cannot betray her."

"She is special to you," Maggie didn't ask but stated.

"Yes. Not the way you assume. Lady L brought her into the organization when she was young. I looked out for her. Became her protector. 'Tis all."

She frowned. "Then why not let Graham help her?"

"Because Lady Langdale will never release her from her clutches without some sort of retaliation. Lady L seeks her revenge against Ravencroft and me because we helped her escape. We even found her a secure place to hide. Only my mother saw her and betrayed her to Lady Langdale."

"Was she the girl at your lodgings the other night?"

"You saw her?"

Maggie laughed. "Ironic, is it not? She dresses like a boy like I do."

Crispin nodded. "One of many of her disguises."

"What is her name?"

"Ren." Crispin paused. "Sabrina."

"That is a pretty name for a pretty girl," Maggie commented.

"Ren is a friend, nothing more," Crispin insisted.

"I believe you. But why must we keep her a secret?"

"Because I promised her I would. She is my inside source for information. Ren has promised to inform me of Lady L's moves."

"Why won't you tell Graham about her?"

"Because your brother's intent with Ren does not lie with the investigation, but concerns a personal interest. He is unaware of the many facets of Ren."

Maggie's lips puckered. "He wishes to act as a rake. Well then, this is one secret I will enjoy keeping from him."

Crispin roared with laughter at her mischievous vindictiveness. Maggie's eyes widened, and she covered his mouth with her hand. In response, he slowly drew each finger into his mouth. Maggie sighed at the wondrous sensation. She hoped Reese would procure them a special license because she couldn't last much longer without having Crispin make love to her.

Soon Crispin's lips were upon hers once more. Soft, slow kisses consumed them. Each time their passion built to a higher level, Crispin would pull back and whisper his intentions into her ear of how he would love her once they married. A day Maggie eagerly waited for.

She never imagined her season would end with a marriage. She only thought to pacify her mother and return home to Worthington Hall after the season ended, to idle her days away on horseback. Instead, she had fallen for a man who made her whole, a soul mate to spend an eternity with. While her family protected her from the harsh realities of life and gave her all the love a girl could ever wish for, the life Crispin led was the complete opposite. Maggie hoped to gift him the happiness he deserved.

Crispin watched Maggie fall asleep, and his hold tightened. She made his heart skip a beat even while she slept. He never wanted to let her go. He didn't think he would ever find someone to love him with the baggage he carried from his past and the demons he had to fight to stay sane. But Maggie surprised him at every turn. Her openness to love without fear amazed him. He never knew what to expect from her and he eagerly waited for tomorrow to see where their love would lead them. Crispin may never deserve Maggie, but he would cherish and love her with all his heart each and every day.

It took a gentle soul to love one whose past had scarred them greatly.

Epilogue

CRISPIN WAS USUALLY A cynical man, but Maggie made him want to quote poems and carry out silly traditions. Which led him to carry her over the threshold at their disposal. Maggie's mother had secured them a suite of rooms at Mivart's for a week to celebrate their wedding. Maggie's laughter followed them inside.

"Crispin, put me down. Your ribs are still sore."

"Shh, I must carry my wife over the threshold. 'Tis a tradition."

Maggie continued her badgering. "Well, we are over the threshold, husband, now set me down."

Crispin's answer was to toss her on the bed. Her skirts flew around her, making her giggle harder. She was incorrigible. Adorable. Sexy as hell. When she curled her finger at him, he went to her willingly. Along the way, he started stripping off his clothes. He had waited anxiously for this night, and he refused to waste another second to make love to Maggie.

Maggie's laughter soon turned into a moan. Crispin's antics warmed her heart, but the desire blazing from his eyes set her soul on fire. He had played the patient for a week under her mother's maternal care; now he was a groom with a purpose.

One Maggie wanted him to fulfill with haste. She was as impatient as Crispin for this night.

"Mrs. Dracott, I believe you wear too much clothing."

"Mmm. Sorry, Mr. Dracott, my husband distracted me."

He shook his head in disappointment, pulling at her legs. He drew her to the edge of the bed and tugged off her shoes, throwing them over his shoulders. Then he slipped her silken stockings off. A sinful smile lit his face.

"Now we are making progress." His lips trailed a path of fire up her legs.

Maggie gasped at the intense pleasure. Surely she would combust from his exquisite kisses. However, she only turned into a puddle of wantonness. She spread her legs, inviting him to love her.

And love her he did. All night and into the next day. Each time was more magical than the last. The outside world waited for them. They still had many obstacles to overcome before they settled into their blissful life. Crispin needed to find his missing brother, and Maggie needed to help her sister heal a broken heart. And they had a villainess to capture. But for now, they only existed in a moment of time designated for themselves.

Tomorrow could wait. They only wished to live for today.

Read Noel & Ravencroft's story in
The Seductive Temptress

"Thank you for reading The Tempting Minx. Gaining exposure as an independent author relies mostly on word-of-mouth, so if you have the time and inclination, please consider leaving a short review wherever you can."

Want to join my mailing list? Visit
www.lauraabarnes.com/contact-newsletter today!

Desire other books to read by Laura A. Barnes

Enjoy these other historical romances:

Fate of the Worthingtons Series
The Tempting Minx
The Seductive Temptress
The Fiery Vixen
The Siren's Gentleman

Matchmaking Madness Series
How the Lady Charmed the Marquess
How the Earl Fell for His Countess
How the Rake Tempted the Lady
How the Scot Stole the Bride
How the Lady Seduced the Viscount
How the Lord Married His Lady

Tricking the Scoundrels Series:
Whom Shall I Kiss... An Earl, A Marquess, or A Duke?
Whom Shall I Marry... An Earl or A Duke?
I Shall Love the Earl
The Scoundrel's Wager
The Forgiven Scoundrel

Romancing the Spies Series:
Rescued By the Captain
Rescued By the Spy
Rescued By the Scot

About Author Laura A. Barnes

International selling author Laura A. Barnes fell in love with writing in the second grade. After her first creative writing assignment, she knew what she wanted to become. Many years went by with Laura filling her head full of story ideas and some funny fish songs she wrote while fishing with her family. Thirty-seven years later, she made her dreams a reality. With her debut novel *Rescued By the Captain*, she has set out on the path she always dreamed about.

When not writing, Laura can be found devouring her favorite romance books. Laura is married to her own Prince Charming (who for some reason or another thinks the heroes in her books are about him) and they have three wonderful children and two sweet grandbabies. Besides her love of reading and writing, Laura loves to travel. With her passport stamped in England, Scotland, and Ireland; she hopes to add more countries to her list soon.

While Laura isn't very good on the social media front, she loves to hear from her readers. You can find her on the following platforms:

You can visit her at ***www.lauraabarnes.com*** to join her mailing list.

Website: https://www.lauraabarnes.com/

Amazon: https://amazon.com/author/lauraabarnes

Goodreads: https://www.goodreads.com/author/show/16332844.Laura_A_Barnes

Facebook: https://www.facebook.com/AuthorLauraA.Barnes/

Instagram: https://www.instagram.com/labarnesauthor/

Twitter: https://twitter.com/labarnesauthor

BookBub: https://www.bookbub.com/profile/laura-a-barnes

TikTok: https://www.tiktok.com/@labarnesauthor

Manufactured by Amazon.ca
Bolton, ON